Love Don't Last Anyways 2

Trinity

Love Don't Last Anyways 2

Copyright © 2015 by Trinity

www.shanpresents.com

Acknowledgments

Acknowledgement

First and foremost, I would like to thank God for giving me a gift to write and explore my creative mind.

Thank you to Shan for giving me countless opportunities. You are truly inspiring and a blessing.

To everyone who supports me, I appreciate it, and I hope you guys continue to enjoy the books I put out.

To my daughter, I can't wait for your arrival. You're the reason I do everything that I do. I love you, baby girl and can't wait until you're here.

To my love, we have been through so much, yet we still stand strong. You've always been my number one supporter, and I appreciate that. Can't wait to see what the future holds, as we continue to build it.

Thank you to my family who is always there for me and who have supported me, nonstop. It's appreciated.

Text Shan to 22828 to stay up to date with new releases, sneak peeks, contest, and more...

Check your spam if you don't receive an email thanking you for signing up.

Table of Contents

Kayla

When I got on the plane, heading to Texas, I didn't look back at my relationship with Melo. My parents were waiting for me at the airport, and I ran straight into their arms and cried. I was so close with them before everything had happened, and I missed them so much. It was a month later, and I missed Briah and felt terrible about the way I treated her. I didn't want to seem selfish, but I had my own reasons to break away from her. I got some therapy to help me heal from losing my daughter.

At first, I placed blame on everyone else, but I realized it wasn't Carmelo's fault; I was sure that he was grieving, too. However, I knew that being with him wasn't a good idea, nor was it healthy. I made a hard decision that I was going go back to Georgia to finish school and be there for Briah and the baby. She didn't have any family, and I, actually, enjoyed going to school there before all the drama had happened. I really missed the days when it was me, Briah, and Jade. I knew that telling my parents that I was going back would make them upset, but there was something about Melo. They didn't like him, and I couldn't understand why. My parents were sitting in the living room, when I decided to break the news.

"Hey, Ma and Dad. I need to talk to you guys," I said, sitting down.

"What's wrong pumpkin?" My dad asked.

"I've decided to go back to Georgia."

"Why?" My mom asked, rolling her eyes.

"I enjoy going to school there, and I really want to be there for Briah and the baby."

"I understand, but you think that's going help your healing process?" My mother asked.

"Yes, I am over what happened, I am not over losing my baby, and don't worry, I have no plans to reconcile with Carmelo."

I assured them. "Well, that's good to hear. I trust you, and I know Briah will be excited to have you there for her and the baby."

"Yup, but don't worry, I'll be here until July." I said, smiling.

"That's great. Maybe you can hang out with Jason."

"Mother, I have no interest in dating anyone. Jason and I have grown apart." I told them. I didn't want anyone to control my life, anymore, and once I got back to Georgia, I was going to make sure of that.

Jade

Although, I was exposed to fresh air while in rehab, to actually walk out of those gates sober, with a clear mind, made a huge difference. As promised, Scott was standing next to a car, waiting for me. He was dressed differently than he was when he was in rehab, though. He had on a crew neck shirt, burgundy shorts, and a pair of Gucci loafers. He looked like he should have been on the cover of a magazine, instead of waiting for me.

"Scott!" I screamed, running up to him, almost knocking him down.

"Jade, I am so happy to see you." he said.

"Same here." I told him.

He opened the door for me, and then, he got in the car.

"So, are you ready?"

"I am. I feel amazing." I said, smiling.

"I can tell. I am so happy for you."

"Thank you, Scott. I really appreciate everything."

"Not a problem. I have a full itinerary for you."

"You do?" I asked, surprised.

"Yes, I need you to get to know Paris if this is going be your temporary home."

"I guess so. So, will you be my tour guide?" I asked.

"I have a lot of catch-up work to do since rehab." he joked.

"I get it. I am not comfortable around strangers."

"Don't worry. I have a few models there who will make sure you enjoy it."

"Okay."

A month later…

Since I entered Paris, my life had changed. Scott was able to be my tour guide for the first two days, and we were able to get to know one another outside of rehab, but on a friendship level. I, also, bonded with one of the models, named Italy, who had worked with them for years. I already booked my first magazine cover, and I was doing my first fashion show. I was nervous, because I felt like I was going fall on my face. I called my brother, Ricky, for advice, because he was the only one in the family that would talk to me. My dad was embarrassed that he couldn't protect me.

"Hello."

"Brother?" I said, smiling, trying not to cry. I missed having a relationship with my brother.

"Jade, baby, how are you?" he asked.

"I am okay. I am in Paris." "Paris, baby girl. What you doing there?" he asked. I told him about Scott and the agency.

"Be safe, baby sis. I don't want anything else to happen to you."

"I will, Ricky, and when I find some time, I will be there to visit you."

4

"I hope so. I can't wait to see you." "Me, too, Ricky. I just called to tell you that I am walking in a fashion show."

"Congrats, sis. I love you."

"I love you, too." I said, hanging up.

I walked back into the dressing room, nervous as hell. Some models were doing their hair and make-up, and there were two in the corner snorting coke. As nervous as I was feeling, it was tempting to go over there. I grabbed a bottle of water and made my way over to the models snorting coke. Maybe a hit would ease my nerves.

Briah

I had been walking around all day trying to get my water to break. Kayla had been here for a few weeks, and she had been really helpful.

"Kayla, why won't this baby come out?" I cried, as we walked through our complex.

"They always say pregnancy teaches you patience. He's going to come out when he's ready." She said, trying to cheer me up. "Whatever, Kayla." I said, catching an attitude.

"Briah, I sure wish Quan's ass was here, so you can be mean to him, since he knocked you up." she said, joking.

"Whatever, I haven't thought about that nigga in forever." I lied.

I thought about Quan every day, and it hurt for him not to be here to go through this with me, but I was beyond thankful for 3T and glad that nothing turned sexual for us. He was super helpful, and I appreciated everything that he did.

"So, what about this rich lawyer that's old enough to be our daddy?" She said, laughing.

"He is just super cool, and he's been there for me."

"Yeah, okay, you sure that's it?"

"Yup, for now. I am not screwing him while I'm pregnant. I am not trifling."

"Shit, that's a fine ass man, and he always smells good." she said, laughing.

"He does girl. My hormones already on 10, and when he comes around, my panties get soaked just thinking about him." I said, causing us both to laugh.

"Kay, you should stay at the condo with me and the baby."

"Really. I was going to go back to the dorms."

"Why?"

"Because, that was my only option."

"Well, you know I want you here, and I need help."

"Poor baby going to have two mamas." I said, joking.

"Sure is." Kayla said, as we walked back into the condo. Kayla sat on the couch, and I took a nap.

I woke up an hour later, with a pain that I had never felt.

"Kay!" I yelled, and another sharp pain came through.

Kayla ran in. "Are you okay?" she asked.

"No. I think it's time." I said, trying to get off the bed, but another sharp pain hit my stomach. "Ughhh!" I screamed. When I stood up, I felt something trickling down my leg.

"Ewww, chick, what is that?" Kayla said.

"Bitch, my water broke. Let's go. I don't have much time." I snapped, not meaning to.

Kayla grabbed my hospital bag, and we headed to the hospital. I was afraid that I was going have my baby in the car, but I prayed that he waited until we got to the hospital. Kayla pulled in front of the hospital and ran in to get two nurses to come back to help me, while she parked the car. They rushed me into the hospital, and while they were checking my vitals, Kayla came up.

"I called Lauren, and they should be on their way."

"I know one thing. This baby is on its way. You're already at eight centimeters." My doctor said.

"So, it's too late for me to get an epidural?" I asked. "Yes, it's going take a minute to prep you for it, and it may slow down the process." The doctor explained.

I was freaking out, the contractions were killing me, and it felt like I was going to need a new pussy. If Quan was here, I would've killed him and brought him back to life.

"Don't worry, Briah. I am here." Kayla said, comforting me.

The pain was killing me, and I couldn't wait for that to be over, because I was never doing that shit, again. An hour later, the doctor informed me that he saw the head, and that it was time to push. I grabbed Kayla's hand and began pushing like my life depended on it. After five pushes, my son came out crying, and I was relieved that it was all over.

"Briah, I am so proud of you." Kayla said.

An hour later, the nurses brought the baby back, and when I looked at him, he had every single feature of Quan's. I named him Chance Brian Harris. I knew Quan wasn't in his life, but I decided to give him his last name.

3T walked in holding balloons, "Congratulations, lil' mama." he said, kissing me on the forehead.

"Thank you."

"He's adorable."

"Thank you, God Dad," I told him.

I had decided to make 3T his godfather, because Chance needed a strong male figure in his life, and 3T had been there for every appointment. He had even helped me find a place for us.

"Wow. I'll take that with honor. Can I hold him?" he asked.

"Sure." I watched him get up and wash his hands, and then, he sat down and held Chance like a natural.

"You're a natural." I said, smiling.

"I do have three kids and two grands," he said, joking.

"B?" I heard someone screech, and I knew it was Lauren. I smiled at the sight of her, until I saw Melo and Quan.

Jade

As I began walking towards the models who were snorting coke, I heard someone call my name. I turned around to a smiling Scott, and I, instantly, felt bad at the thought of wanting to snort.

"Jade, you ready?" he asked.

"Very nervous." I told him.

"You're going to do fine. Trust me, I just needed you to have confidence in yourself." he said, smiling.

He was right. I needed to prove to myself that I could do it and that I wasn't wasting my time. Scott gave me a second chance and I owed it to him and myself not to mess things up. I took a swig of water and got into the model line. I could hear people clapping, but my mind was on not embarrassing myself. I walked with the other models, with confidence, knowing that my addiction wouldn't win. I no longer felt like I didn't have the confidence, as people were clapping while I walked in. The bright lights and smiles of strangers caused a high that I had never felt before. I no longer craved cocaine; I craved fame.

Briah

"B?" Lauren said, with all smiles, walking into the room, not knowing how much tension she had just caused by bringing Melo and Quan with her.

"Hey L," I said, trying to ignore the two figures.

"Really, Briah? This the shit you pull?" Quan snapped.

"What are you talking about, Quan?" I said, with an attitude.

"You know exactly what I am talking about."

"Hey, Melo." I said, ignoring Quan.

"Ain't no hey Melo." Quan snapped.

"Look, she just had a baby. She doesn't need to deal with this." 3T said, standing up for me.

"Look, Briah, tell your pops to mind his business."

"Listen, young bull, I am not her father."

"Well, what the hell you doing here, unless her hoe ass telling you that you the papi?"

"Quan, enough!" Lauren, yelled.

"Nah, L, you stopped me from watching strippers shaking their asses and was coming at my neck, talking about how I wasn't there for Briah and my seed, but we get to the hospital, and Daddy Warbucks here is holding her son. I am out." He said, leaving the room. I was happy that he had left.

"Briah, I am really sorry. I had no idea that you didn't want him here. I just got mad that he was watching bitches shake their asses, while my lil' sis gave birth to his baby."

"It's cool, L."

"Good. I want to see my nephew." she said, smiling. She washed her hands, and 3T gave her the baby.

"Briah, I have to go. I'll come check on you guys." 3T said, kissing my forehead and walking out.

"Briah, you good?" Lauren asked.

"Yes, I am fine. I am not dealing with Quan and his mess." I said, holding back tears that I didn't know I had.

Kayla

I thought that seeing Melo was going to bring back my feelings for him, but it didn't. I guess that was because I was still bitter about losing my baby. I left the room and allowed Lauren to console Briah, since she caused that mess. I am sure that she didn't mean any harm, but Quan knew that he was wrong for the way he treated Briah. I decided to go to the café across from the hospital and get something to eat. When I sat in an empty booth and looked at the menu, I noticed a figure staring at me, but I continued to scan my options, trying my hardest to ignore him. My waitress came over and took my order, and when she left, the gentleman who was staring at me walked over.

I had butterflies in my stomach and became nervous, because I hadn't even thought about men, and this guy in front of me was fine.

"Can I join you?" he asked, sitting down.

"I guess. You already sat down." I said, smirking.

"I couldn't help but wonder why a woman as beautiful as you would be eating alone." he said, showing his perfect pearly whites.

"Just a quick meal." I said, blushing.

"If you were my woman, you wouldn't be here alone." he said, with force that turned me on.

It was something about that man that melted me. He was tall, around six-four, with ripped muscles, light skin, a bald head, and a full beard. It was something about that man that screamed dangerous, but I couldn't help but to be intrigued.

"I guess." I told him.

"What's your name, dimples?" he asked.

"Kayla."

"Sweet Kay." he said, causing me to blush. "I see you like to show those dimples. My name is Derrick." he said, holding out his hand. My waitress brought my food to the table, but I didn't want to eat, anymore. I wanted to stare and talk to Derrick. "Well, pretty lady, I just wanted to let you know how beautiful you were looking over here." he said, getting up.

"Why don't you join me?" I said.

"Sure." he said, as he sat back down.

For the next hour, we talked about pretty much everything. I found out that he was 30, owned a few businesses, he didn't have any children, nor was he in relationship. After our conversation, I went back to the hospital to see Briah, and Derrick and I agreed to meet up at another time.

Jade

"Jade, you killed the runway." Scott said, with excitement.

"Thank you. I was super nervous." I said, with a slight laugh.

"I can't tell. You were a natural."

"Thanks, Scott." I wanted to tell him about me almost slipping up, but I didn't want to let him down. I wanted to do any and everything to make him proud and prove that I can do better than before.

"What are your plans for later?" Scott asked.

"Sleep." I said. I was so exhausted the modeling on the runway took hours of practice and prep time.

Two years later...

Kayla

"Kayla Monroe," the announcer said.

I walked across the stage and heard loud cheers. I looked across the room and noticed the proud faces of my parents. Briah, and Derrick displayed that I was, officially, a college graduate with a degree in Early Childhood. The last two years had been filled with ups and downs, as well as good times. The best thing about it was watching my god-son grow. After I received my diploma, we all headed to dinner.

"Kay, I am so proud of you." Briah said.

"I agree, Kayla. You make me and your father so proud." My mother said, smiling.

"Thank you." I said.

"I know my baby is going be a dope teacher." Derrick said, holding me with a tight embrace.

"Thank you." I said, with a faint smile.

"So, Kayla, what's next? Are you coming back to Texas?" My mother asked.

"I haven't decided, yet. I think I want to stay here." I told them.

We ate dinner and made more small talk. On the way out, we literally, bumped into Melo and a brown-skinned chick walking hand-in-hand. My stomach still did flips at the sight of him.

"Congrats, Kayla." he said, smiling, then he spoke to Briah and Chance.

I said good-bye to my parents, and Briah and I got in the car with Derrick, and as soon as I did, I was greeted by a smack.

"How dare you disrespect me like that?" I held my face, in shock, because this was Derrick's thing.

"Dee, what did I do?" I asked, confused.

"Still talking to that nigga, huh?" he said.

"He congratulated me. I didn't want to be rude." I snapped.

"Watch, when we get home," he said, starting the car and driving off.

I knew that it was about to be a long night. My only fear was facing my parents tomorrow with a battered face, but I was hoping that, this time, he didn't do it. I said a silent prayer the entire ride home. Once we got home, he didn't say anything, so I figured that he had forgot. I took a shower and laid in the bed, drifting off to sleep when I was awakened by a whip with a belt.

"What the hell?!" I screamed, jumping up to Derrick trying to beat me.

"You not going to embarrass me anymore." he shouted, with venom in his eyes.

"I didn't, I swear." I pleaded.

Derrick had been beating my ass for the past six months; he had become extremely jealous, and the thought of Melo and I would send him over the edge. I hadn't spoken to Melo in, close to, three years, and Derrick didn't get that I just didn't want Melo. I wasn't over him, but the thought of my child being killed, purposely, was something I could never forget.

Jade

"Just like that." Red, my photographer, said.

I posed on a bike, showing off my assets. Modeling had been good to me, and I was becoming a household name.

"Good job, baby." Jared, my boyfriend, said walking over to me.

"Thank you." I said, walking over to him, giving him a kiss.

Jared and I met a year ago; he became my manager, and then, we began dating. Jared was ten years older than me, and he resembled Blair Underwood. It was as if they could be twins.

"I got a surprise for you tonight, at dinner." he said, excitingly.

"Thank you, babe."

"Jade, you know you deserve it." He said, giving me a forehead kiss, causing me to blush. I finished my shoot and had my car brought to me. While I was waiting, I used the time to check my emails. I had an urgent email, from Scott, to call him. Since, I had met Jared, Scott and I had, kind of, become distant. I called Scott, immediately.

"Hello, my favorite money maker." He joked.

I didn't think he was joking, because I was making his company a lot of money. "Hey, Scott, what's up?" I asked.

"I really didn't want anything, but I am in California and wanted to hang out, tonight."

"Awe, Scott. I am sorry. Jared has a surprise dinner for me."

"Okay, Jade, I have to go." He said, hanging up.

I didn't know what his problem was, but I had no patience to babysit a grown man. I entered my spacious condo, proud of myself. Three years ago, I was strung out on drugs, with no future. Now, I was one of the hottest models, with an amazing boyfriend. My mother refused to talk to me, though. My dad tried his hardest to talk to me. Ricky and I tried to talk, often, but he was married with a new baby. I didn't have any friends in my life. It only consisted of Jared and modeling.

Sometimes, I thought about Kayla and Briah and what our friendship could have been. Jared texted me and let me know a car would be waiting for me at seven. I checked the time, and it was already five. I took a quick shower, because I knew it was going to take me forever to find an outfit. Once I got out the shower, I chose a white pencil skirt, with a peach baby doll top. On my feet, were a pair of Peach Louboutin, strap-on shoes, and I accessorized with a little gold jewelry. My hair was in a short pixie cut, which outlined my round face. My makeup was light, and I choose a peach color for my lips.

Once I was done, it was pass seven, and I had a ton of missed calls. I grabbed my bag, ran out and apologized to the driver, numerous times. But, he didn't seem to mind. We pulled up to my favorite Cuban restaurant and the driver let me out. I figured that Jared was going to pull out all of the stops. The hostess recognized me, because I was always there.

"Follow me, Ms. Jade." she said, smiling.

I spotted Jared, sitting down, sipping some Jack Daniels looking dapper.

"I already ordered your food; I knew you were going be late." he said, laughing.

"You know me well." I said.

"Well, how was your day?" he asked.

"Things were okay, and yours?" I asked.

"Very busy. I have a job opportunity in Atlanta." I, immediately, tensed up. Atlanta wasn't a good place for me, and I didn't know what that meant for us.

"Really?" I said, taking a sip of wine.

"Yes, but I want you to come with me."

"My life is here." I told him.

"Is it really? Your career is here, but I am ready to be a family." I knew this conversation would come up, eventually. He was older than me, and men got tired of the same lifestyle. "This is why I bought this." He said, taking a box out of his pocket and placing it on the table. My eyes grew wide.

"What's going on?" I asked, nervously.

"Jade, will you marry me?" he asked.

"Yes." I said. I was in love, and he was right. I longed for a man in my life that showed me the way women should be treated.

Kayla

The next morning, I woke up to a diamond bracelet. That was Derrick's motto; he would hit me, and then, bribe me with things. I was terrified of leaving him. My parents loved him, and I loved him, too, but I wasn't in love with him anymore. I felt like I was falling down a path of living but not really living.

I was starting a new job at a school, and it had always been my dream to teach. I was getting second graders, and I was nervous, because I felt like I was still young and would be bossing the kids around. It was my first day, and I wanted to make a good impression, so I decided to a wear a black Gucci pencil skirt, with a pink Gucci Chiffon shirt. I accessorized with my grandmother's pearls. On my feet, I chose a pair of beige Michael Kors wedges that I knew would be comfortable, because I was going to be doing a lot of walking. I put my hair in a tight bun and applied light make-up. I looked at myself in the mirror and knew I was beautiful, but being a women who was abused, I was often scared to over dress.

I walked down the stairs and Derrick was sitting at the kitchen table eating a muffin and reading the paper, like nothing had happened.

"Good morning." I said.

"Morning, babe. You look good for your first day. I hope I don't have to fuck those little niggas up." He said, smirking, but knowing his crazy ass, he meant what he said.

I let out a laugh, kissed him on the cheek, and made my way to work. When I arrived to John F Kennedy Elementary, I had butterflies. I was greeted by the security guard.

"Good morning, Ms. Lady." he said, with a heavy African accent.

"Good morning." I said, looking down, even though Derrick wasn't around. Making eye contact with a man was a no-no.

I was in search of the principal, Mrs. Greene, but before I could find her, she found me.

"Ms. Monroe, I've been waiting for you, how are you?" she asked, with a warm smile.

There was something about her that was warm and inviting.

"I am okay… nervous."

"Don't be. The kids will love you. I've placed you in Room 114. Follow me. I can show you where it is." she said.

I followed her and admired the art work that the children had created. I knew this was my calling, and I was doing the right thing by taking this job.

"Room 114. Now, if you need anything, don't hesitate to call me. The kids will arrive in about twenty minutes." she told me.

I had about fifteen minutes to unwind, so I wrote the notes on the board and straightened up, to my liking, when the bell rang. Kids begin to pile in, so I walked to the door to greet the rest of my second graders. Once everyone was seated, I took attendance and was only missing one student.

"Okay, class. I am Ms. Monroe." I was interrupted by a knock on the door. I looked up and had to hold my composure. "Excuse me, boys and girls." I told them, walking to the door.

"Kayla!" Cameron screeched. I hadn't seen Carmelo's son in almost two years.

"Hi, Cam, how are you?" I asked.

"I am okay. Are you my teacher?" he asked, with excitement.

"Yes, I am, so when you're in school, I need you to call me, Ms. Monroe" I told him, in a whisper.

"Okay."

"Cameron, can you go sit down with your classmates," I told him.

Looking at Carmelo made me nervous; he seemed like he got better with age, and he cut his braids off. His waves were, definitely, making me cream.

"Well, Kay, I am proud of you." he said, with a smile.

"Thanks, can you please bring him at a better time?" I told him.

"My bad. I was told last minute to bring him here." he said.

"Yeah, I know how Dana can be, but anyway, I have to go."

"See ya' later." He said, leaving.

I knew that Cameron being in my class was going be a problem, especially, with Derrick. I just prayed that he didn't find out and that he kept his hands to himself.

Briah

Having my son gave me a new outlook on life. I hadn't seen, Quan since the day he barged into the hospital, and then, left. I was, actually, at peace with him not being around. It had been two years, and I was a different person. 3T really helped me a lot; I was still working for him, while going to school. He also helped me with Chance. That day, he was taking me to lunch, because we hadn't seen each other in a while.

I walked through our favorite Cuban restaurant, and he was sitting at the table, dressed to impress and on his phone. Although he was in his late 50's, that man was beyond fine. I was happy that we never took it there, but there were some days I wished we had.

"Hey 3?" I said, kissing him on the cheek and sitting down.

"Hey, Briah. How are you, and how's Chance?" he asked.

"Everything is everything." He replied.

"How was Jersey?" I asked, trying not to pry.

"Divorce is final. It's been a long five years." He said, with a smile, taking a sip of his drink. Deep down, I was relieved that he had, finally, got his divorce.

"Well, whatever, makes you happy." I replied.

The waitress came, placing our food on the table. We frequented the restaurant, often, so I knew 3 was going to order for me.

"My man, 3." We heard someone say, causing us both to look up.

"Hey, Jared. How is it going?" 3T asked, shaking his hand.

"Great. I am moving down here and getting married." the guy told him.

"Well, congrats, man. This is my friend, Briah. Briah, this is my boy, Jared. I use to mentor him." 3T said, introducing us.

"Nice to meet you." I said, with a smile.

"Jared, you ready?" a voice asked. I turned, and it was Jade.

"Jade?" I said, shocked.

"Briah?" she said, looking just as shocked as me.

"You guys know each other?" Jared asked.

"We use to be college roommates." I replied.

"See, babe, and you were worried that you didn't have anyone here."

By the look on Jade's face, I was not sure that he knew the full extent of her problems, in Atlanta, but if she wanted to hide it, it wasn't my place to rehash old wounds.

"Well, how about you give me your number, and we can do lunch and catch up?" I said, trying to break her uneasy feeling.

"That's fine." she said, pulling out her iPhone.

We exchanged numbers, and then, said our goodbyes. Once they left, 3T was staring at me.

"What happened?" I asked.

"I am proud you. I know what you guys been through."

"Well, that's water under the bridge. We're both grown, now." I told him.

For the rest of the lunch, we just caught up. I had to leave, because Lauren was watching Chance, and I didn't want her to feel like she was babysitting for too long. I, also, envied driving up to Black and Lauren's mansion. They were hood billionaires who loved us all and who I admired. They had heavy security, because Black was well-known, and a lot of people were always out to harm him.

I had to text Lauren to see where she was in the house, because the house was so big. She texted me back and told me that she was in the family room, in the south wing. I knew I was in for a journey, so I made a brief run to her bathroom, but someone was in it. I gave them two more minutes. I could hear the person spraying, which meant that they took a shit, and I had to deal with it, especially, because my bladder was going to burst. When Quan opened that door, I felt a little pee trickle down.

"Briah, what your trick ass doing here?"

"Whatever. Excuse me, funky." I said, trying to get pass him.

"I forgot you be stripping and hustling for Black." he said, smirking.

"Gotta feed my son."

"How is your son? You still got your grandfather playing daddy?"

"Whatever." I told him, getting pass him, to hold my breath and use the bathroom.

I prayed that, once I got out the bathroom, he would be gone. Just like I thought, he was no longer there, so I went to the playroom and found Black, Lauren, Chance, and Quan. The adults were in a deep conversation, and Chance was focused on his iPad.

"Here goes the trick now" Quan spat.

"Quan, chill." Lauren said.

"You a trick, too, helping her keep my son away from me."

"Quan, watch it. You know I don't play that disrespectful shit."

"Can we use different words?" I said, becoming annoyed, pointing at Chance.

Lauren got headphones off the desk and put them in Chance's ears.

"Quan, you need to relax, instead, of coming at her like that." Lauren said, coming to my defense.

"Why should I?"

"If I am not mistaken, you came to the hospital when I had him, and then, you left. I don't have your contact information, so I, damn sure, wasn't going to chase you." I spat.

"Look, you had that old nigga in there. I thought he was your sugar daddy."

"Well, he's not. He's someone that helped me when I was pregnant and homeless." I said, trying to fight back the tears.

"Man, whatever." Quan said, storming off.

"That's your problem. Always storming off, especially, when things get tough." I said.

"Let him go, Bri. He's such a jackass."

"L, mind ya' business." Black said to her, with a stern look.

"Why was Quan here?" I asked.

"He's Black's son. Today, Black was going tell him." Lauren said, looking at Black.

I couldn't believe that. Quan thought he didn't have a father, but it started to make sense on why Black was so close to Chance. Every time I got Quan out of my system, he came back.

Jade

I sat across from my parents, playing in my food. We were at Ricky's for dinner, and I didn't want Jared to come in and get wrapped up in my dysfunctional family. The crazy part was that it wasn't always that way.

"So, Jade, how's the modeling?" Ricky's wife, Savanah, asked.

"It's going good." I said, trying to keep it short.

"I buy every magazine and show you off." My dad said, boosting my ego and making me feel good.

"So, sis, I can't believe you're moving back here."

"Yes, I was kind of skeptical, but Jared insisted, and I can just travel to work when I need to."

"Well, good for you." My mother said.

"Well, thanks, mom. You hadn't said a word, but hi, to me."

"I am scared to talk. I may get blamed for something else." she said, sarcastically.

"Really, Ma?" I said, slamming my fork down.

"Relax, ladies, please." Ricky said.

"Look, I am getting married in two weeks, and this is the reason I didn't bring my husband. I want to start a new life, with no drama." I said, in tears.

"Sis, really, if he makes you happy, I am happy for her, but you know you have to bring him around, so I can approve." Ricky said, trying to lighten up the mood.

"I'll do that. We're not having a big wedding; we're, actually, just going do the courthouse thing." I said, nonchalantly.

"Really, baby girl? I always dreamed of walking you down the aisle." My father said.

I loved my father, but he was so far up my mother's ass, that he ruined our father-daughter relationship. I thought about all the father-daughter dances we attended and all the football games we would watch together. A tear escaped my eye, and I, quickly, wiped it, before they could see it.

"Well, Jade, you and your husband can meet up with Ricky and me for lunch." Savannah said, trying to break the ice.

"Yeah, sis, next week sound good?" Ricky asked.

"Perfect." I told them.

The rest of the dinner went well me, and my mother and I ignored one another. I couldn't wait to get home and cuddle with Jared. After the awkward dinner, I headed home. Jared was sitting on the couch, watching ESPN.

"Hey, babe." I said, slipping my shoes off.

"How was dinner?" he asked.

"Interesting."

"Well, I got some good news. I was able to pull some strings, and we can get married tomorrow."

"Tomorrow?" I said, surprised.

"Yeah, you don't wanna marry me?" he asked.

"I do, but I didn't know it would be so soon."

"Why wait when you're in love?" he said, kissing me.

"Your right. Well, isn't it bad luck to see the bride the night before?" I asked.

"We don't need luck when we have each other."

"You're right." I walked upstairs and prepped a bath; I just wanted to relax.

My phone rang, before I got in the water, and I only answered, because it was Scott.

"Hello"

"Well, hello to you, too, Ms. Jade." Scott said.

"Hi Scott. How may I help you?" I said, irritated. Lately, it been on one and I didn't have time. "Well did you forget you have a job?" he asked.

"Of course I didn't. I'll be flying out to Paris in three weeks." No matter how much I loved Jared, my career meant everything to me, and I was going to finish all of my projects.

"Okay, good. How's Atlanta?" he asked.

"It's good. We're getting married, tomorrow."

"So soon?"

"Scott, please don't start."

"Okay, Jade. Good luck, and see you in three weeks." he said, hanging up. I brushed him off and got in the tub.

The next day, I got up with butterflies, excited to become Mrs. Jared Grant. I looked through my suitcase and didn't have anything fit for a wedding, nor did I have time to shop.

"Good morning, beautiful." Jared said, walking in smiling.

"I can't find anything to wear." I complained.

"Babe, you can throw on anything and kill it."

"Yeah, but it's our wedding day, and you know how you dress." I told him.

"I can tone it down a little bit."

"Oh, please, you and I both know you don't know what that means." I said, laughing.

"Just wear a nice, simple Maxi dress. Remember, I am marrying you, not what you wear, and besides, who else can say that they are marrying a super model?" he said, kissing me on my forehead and walking out.

I searched in my suitcase and chose a plain black Maxi dress. It was plain, but it complimented my figure. I knew that the tradition was something new, borrowed, and blue, but right now, I didn't have the time to worry about traditions. Hopefully, Jared and I could start our own. I finished getting dressed and walked downstairs, where Jared was engrossed in his phone.

"Ready?" I asked.

"Of course, I am." I told him, smiling.

We headed to the courthouse hand-in-hand. I was excited for our new beginnings.

Kayla

I loved my job, and my kids were breaths of fresh air, especially, when I had to deal with Derrick's bullshit. I felt like he would really kill me, before he allowed me to leave him. I tutored some of the kid's after school who needed extra help. Carmelo's son, Cameron, was one of them, and I felt like I was sneaking around, because I knew Derrick would have flipped out. While I was going over Cam's grammar, Melo knocked on the door and walked in.

"Daddy." Cameron screamed, running over to him.

I loved the bond that Cameron and Melo had. It made me think about my daughter and what could have been. I, quickly, nixed those feelings, because I didn't want to get emotional.

"Hey, Kay." Carmelo said, smiling.

Carmelo was fine; that was something I couldn't deny.

"Hey, Mel. We're done, right Cam?"

"Yes." he said, packing his belongings.

I packed my bags and Melo and Cam waited for me to lock up.

"You guys didn't have to wait." I told them.

"Nah, you good. You already know what time of person I am." Melo said.

The three of us walked out, and I was surprised to see Derrick standing by my car. Of course, my steps became slower, and my heart begin beating faster. Melo could sense my uneasiness.

"Kayla, you good?" Melo asked.

"I'm fine." I said, keeping my head down.

"So, this is what we do at work?" Derrick screamed, with his arms folded, standing by my car.

"Yo', chill with that yelling shit!" Melo said.

"Mind ya' business, B." Derrick said.

"Come on, Derrick." I said, scared of what was going to happen next.

"Kayla, are you sure you're fine?" Melo asked.

"Yes!" I shouted, not meaning to yell, but Melo had no idea how fucked I was going to be once I got home.

The car ride with Derrick was quicker than usual. Once my feet was planted on the ground, my body moved slowly. Derrick opened the door and pushed me in, causing me to fall.

"You going to stop embarrassing me. Every time that nigga come around, you're in his face." He said, kicking me on the side of my face. My face begin to sting. "Open those legs." Derrick ordered.

"Please don't, Derrick." I cried.

Derrick had abused me, not only, mentally and physically, but sexually, as well. He pulled my skirt up, pushed my panties to the side, and roughly inserted himself. Whenever he did that, it would usually take less than five minutes, and that time was no different. He got off of me and left. I stayed in the same spot and cried. I was living, physically, but my spirit was, mentally, gone. I, finally, managed to pick myself up and climb myself into bed. I knew that Derrick wasn't going come back, until the next day, but I hoped and prayed that he didn't return at all. The next morning, I woke up with a major headache. I didn't want to go to work, but I had no choice, because I hadn't even finished my probationary period yet.

I looked in the mirror and cringed at the red mark on my face, and I knew that it was only a matter of time before my face was going to swell. I, quickly, got dressed, headed to work, and hoped no one noticed. I put makeup on the bruise to cover up the scar. When I arrived to school, Carmelo and Cameron were standing outside the classroom, and they scared the hell out of me.

"Good morning, Kay, I mean, Ms. Monroe." Cameron said.

"Good morning. What are you guys doing here?" I asked.

"We decided to bring you breakfast for helping Cam out." Melo said.

"It's my job." I told him, refusing to make eye contact.

"Well, it's appreciated." Melo said.

I opened the door and begin preparing for the day.

Carmelo was staring at me. "Kayla, are you sure you're okay?" he asked.

"Yes, I am fine." I said, becoming annoyed.

"Look, don't snap on me, because you have shit going on." He snapped.

"Whatever." I told him, waving him off.

"Kayla, this not even you. The Kayla I know is confident and brave. This new one ain't nothing, but weak." He snapped, walking out of the classroom.

His words stung, and I wanted to run out and cry myself to sleep, but I had to put my big girl panties on and get through the day.

Briah

"Wait, Quan doesn't know?" I asked.

"No. Black was going to tell him, today. I guess that seeing you set him off." Laruen explained.

"Quan has a bad attitude." I told them.

"Oh, we know. That little nigga gets on my nerves." Lauren said.

"Wait... Black, Quan thinks his father abandoned him. I think the news is going make him bitter." I told him.

"I know, but it's time I tell him. That's why I treat Chance the way I do. I can tell he's Quan's." Black confessed.

"Well, good luck, Black. I know it won't be easy, and thanks guys for keeping him." I said, saying my good-byes and grabbing Chance.

Once I left, I sat in my car and let out a sigh. Black was Quan's dad, but Quan didn't even believe Chance was his.

A week later, I was sitting at work, bored, when a women walked through the door, fly as hell. She had smooth, mocha skin and was tall and slim, with big brown eyes. Her hair was styled in a cherry bob, and she was dressed to the nines in a cream Gucci pants suit. She wore bright orange, peep-toe Gucci pumps and accessorized her wrist, with a Piaget watch and her Givenchy bag on her right side.

"Excuse me. I am looking for 3," she said.

"He's in a meeting. Can I take a message?" I asked, curious to know who she was.

3 went on a lot of dates with women, but not one of her caliber.

"My name is Jackie Peterson. He knows exactly who I am." She said, with confidence.

"Okay, give me a second." I told her, getting up and knocking on his door.

"Come in."

"You have a Jackie Peterson here." I told him.

His face lit up, and I knew that there was something special about her. He wrapped up his meeting within five minutes and greeted her with a smile.

"Hey, Jackie." 3 said, smiling. The chemistry they had caused me to have a bit of jealousy. I never paid the rest of the women he brought around any mind, because they weren't on his level, but this Jackie Peterson was on different.

"Briah, can you go downstairs and grab us some coffee?" 3 asked.

I was a bit offended, because he was treating me like an assistant in front of this bitch, but of course, I had to do my job. 3 had been nothing but a life saver.

"Okay." I said, memorizing both their coffee orders.

On my way down, I ran into Melo in the elevator.

"Was up, Briah?" He said.

"Hey, Mel. Long time, no see." I said.

"I know. Sorry about barging in the hospital when you had your son." He said.

"I get it. I know whose idea it was."

"But, have you spoken to Kay?" he asked.

"Not since she started working. Why?" I asked, confused.

"Check on her." he said, getting out of the elevator.

Once my floor came, I grabbed the coffee and went back upstairs to give the new lovers their coffee.

"Briah, you can take the rest of the day off." He told me.

"Thanks." I said, smiling.

I grabbed my things and left. I was happy to get out of there. I decided to go do a little retail shopping for Chance and I. While I was in the mall, I saw Quan with bags in his hands. I tried to hide from him, but I knew that he saw me when I heard him yell,

"Aye, trick."

I wanted to fuck him up, but I tried to keep my composure. I walked faster, but he caught up with me.

"Sup' trick or treat." he said, laughing.

"Quan, what the hell do you want?" I snapped.

"I can't say hi to a friend."

"Friends aren't disrespectful." I snapped.

"Whoa, chill out, Briah. You know I like to fuck with you." Quan said, laughing.

"Yeah, but you're just rude as hell."

"Whatever, so what's good with that baby?" he asked. I was surprised that he even asked about Chance.

"You wanna see a picture of him?" I asked.

"Yeah, why not." I pulled out my iPhone and showed Quan a recent picture of Chance. Quan looked at the phone closely.

"Look, you mind if I send this to my phone to show my grandmother?" he asked.

"Show her for what?" I asked, curious even though, I knew why. Chance and Quan looked just like alike.

He gave me his number, and I texted him the picture.

"A'ite, check you later." he said, nonchalantly, walking away.

That was Quan's thing; he would act like he cared one minute, and the next, he didn't.

Quan

Seeing Briah so much, lately, made me change the way I looked at her. When I first met her, she was this fun ghetto chick, but then, things between us just started happening. I also had a lot of problems in the streets during Briah's entire pregnancy, and I was locked up, so I figured that she was better off without me. When Lauren told me that she was giving birth, I had a change of heart, until I saw some strange, older guy holding the baby, so I figured he was the daddy, and I bounced.

Briah was stripping and hustling, so I wasn't sure what kind of shit she was out there doing. Watching her walk in the mall with that fat ass had me missing her young ass. When she showed me a picture of her son, Chance, I knew, right then, that he was mines. I texted my grandmother the picture, right away, and she called me.

"Yes, grandma." I said.

"Laquan Harris, whose child is that?" She yelled.

I knew that she had her hand on her hip. My grandmother was super dramatic.

"It's Briah's, Ma." I said.

"Briah? That little girl you brought here? I figured your hoe ass chased her away."

"Really, grandma?"

"What Quanie? You I and both know how you are."

"Anyway, did you really look at the picture?" I yelled.

"Look, little nigga, don't be yelling at me. I swear, you have anger issues. Yes, I did, and that baby is a Harris. I am giving you and Briah a month to bring that little boy to see his grandmother." She fussed.

"Grandma, I have to talk to Briah."

"Yeah, but leave that attitude at the door. No body going to deal with that bullshit. I swear your parents were both crazy and mean."

"Parents, I thought you didn't know who my pops was?" I said, confused.

"I meant mother, boy."

"Grandma, please cut the bullshit."

"Laquan Harris, I don't know who the fuck you talking to. I ain't ya' hoe ass mama. You and Briah got a month to bring that baby here. Goodbye!" she said, hanging up.

My grandmother really just fucked my head up, talking about my parents. My phone began ringing, and I thought it was her calling back, but it was Black. He had been blowing my phone up worse than a bitch. I was done with the drug game. Between people trying to kill me, and getting locked up, it wasn't worth it. Especially, if Briah's son was mines. I wanted to focus on my realtor business, and maybe, my son. I sent Briah a text asking to meet up. Now that my grandmother was in our business, I knew, for sure, that she would be harassing me about Briah's son, so I had to take care of that ASAP.

Jade

The ceremony between Jared and I went quickly. After we said I do, we went to a sushi bar, and then, Jared had something to do. I decided to stay at the bar and have a few drinks alone, but I was pissed that Jared and I couldn't spend our wedding night together. I decided to just chill in the house for the rest of the day.

I was relaxing on the couch, when my brother, Ricky, called me.

"Hello."

"Hey, sis, congratulations."

"Thanks, Rick."

"Well, Savanah and I wanted to take you guys out to celebrate."

"I would love to, but Jared had work to finish, so I am home just relaxing."

"Okay, well tell that husband of yours that your brother wants to meet him."

"I will. No problem." I said, laughing.

My brother was still overprotective, and it actually felt good to have someone to be that way when it comes to me. When I hung up with Ricky, I received a text from Briah. We had been texting here and there, lately.

Briah: Hey, you want to meet for drinks?

Jade: Sure, what time?
Briah: An hour. I'll text you the place.

I was happy that Briah and I was going to meet, because I didn't have many friends, and I needed to start hanging out and mingling. I slipped my clothes back on and made my way to Xen Lounge, where Briah wanted to meet at. We both arrived at the same time, and I was happy she was on time, because I hated waiting for people.

"Hey, Jade." She said, giving me a hug.

"Hey, boo." I said, taking a seat at the bar.

I was a big Patron drinker, so I ordered a Patron margarita, and Briah ordered Henny on the rocks.

"So, how's mommy hood?" I asked.

"It's good. I am tired of raising him, alone, but other than that, Chance is perfect." She said, smiling.

"I have to meet him."

"You sure do. How is the boyfriend?" she asked.

"Husband." I told her.

"Oh my, really? Congratulations."

"Thank you. We got married this morning." I said, smiling.

"Awe, Jade, no one deserves it more than you." she said, genuinely.

"Thank you. I hope it lasts."

"Oh, it will. Jared seems nice."

"He is. I really love him. What's going on with you and that sexy Idris Elba look alike?" I asked.

"Oh, nothing. He's cool. Really nice, but he doesn't look at me like that."

"I couldn't be around him and not want to jump his bones." I said, laughing.

"Jade, you have no idea. I want to jump his bones. Hell, I am in love with him." She confessed.

"Damn, really?"

"Yup, but I know things won't work."

"Have you seen Quan?"

"Not really. Quan is so ignorant. I can't really deal with him." I said, half-joking.

"I remember his mouth. He's a mess. Anyway, what's Ms. Kay up to?" I asked.

"Kay is good. She just got a new job as a teacher, so we haven't really gotten to see one another." She said.

I could sense a bit of distance between the two of them.

"All three of us have to get together for old time's sake."

"How's my ex-husband, Ricky?" she asked.

"Ricky is good. He's married, now."

"That's dope. He's a great guy."

Briah and I ordered more drinks and caught each other up on our lives. I hoped we could keep our friendship like that, because I missed her and missed having a genuine friend. My legs started to feel like jello, which meant that I had had a little too much to drink. I said my goodbyes and drove home, before I wouldn't be able to. I couldn't wait to get home and fuck my brand new husband. I got excited when I pulled in the driveway, and his car was there. There was another car parked behind his, and I prayed that, whoever it was, wasn't trying to stay any longer, because I wanted to spend time with my husband.

When I got into the house, I spotted two wine glasses on the kitchen counter.

"Jared." I called out. All the lights were off, so I took my shoes off and climbed up the stairs. As I got closer to our bedroom, I heard moans of ecstasy, and my heart began to beat faster. I thought Jared was perfect, and here I was, played again. I ran downstairs and grabbed the gun out of the hallway closet and went back upstairs. I was tired of motherfuckers playing me. I bust through the door and wanted to throw up at the sight of my husband fucking a man that was on all fours.

"Jared?!" I screamed, in disgust and anger.

They both stopped and looked at me. The guy on all fours was his supposed business partner, Darren.

"Jared, baby just tell her the truth."

"Shut up, Darren!" Jared said, trying to get away from Darren.

In a blink of an eye, I shot Darren in the head.

"Jade, baby what did you do?" Jared asked, teary-eyed.

"Leave me alone!" I said, with tears in my eyes, as I shot Jared in the head.

I dropped the gun, walked downstairs, poured a glass of water, and sat at the kitchen table.

Ten minutes later, the police was knocking on the door. I knew they were coming, because I was sure that the neighbors heard the noise and called the police. I didn't move from where I was sitting. The cops bust down the door, and I called Briah.

"Hello." Briah answered, groggily.

"Briah, I killed Jared" I cried.

Kayla

Melo had really cut me with his words, but everything he said was true. I had lost my self-confidence, and I needed a change, because either I was going kill myself, or Derrick was going kill me. I called my mother for some advice, because I was too embarrassed to tell Briah what was going on. I had, actually, been keeping my distance from her.

"Hello, Kayla, how are you?" she asked.

"I am okay."

"Are you sure? You don't sound okay?"

"Derrick and I are going through some issues, and I don't know what to do." I confessed.

"Well, baby, he's a good man, and I think he's great for you. Don't do anything to mess it up."

I couldn't believe my mother. That man was whooping my ass, and she was telling me how good he was. In her eyes, if you wasn't Carmelo, you was good enough.

"I have to go." I said, cutting her off and hanging up. I didn't need a Derrick cheerleader.

I was at such a low point in my life that I just wanted to die. I had pushed everyone away and felt like I had nothing else left in me. It was a Saturday, so my plans were to chill around the house. Derrick was on a business trip, so I had the house to myself. I was catching up on reality TV, when the doorbell rang. I didn't expect any visitors, so I was a little surprised. I opened the door and was greeted by Briah and Chance.

"Hey, stranger." She said, smiling and walking in.

"Hey, boo." I said, picking up Chance and holding him close.

"So, what are you guys doing here?" I asked.

"We can't come visit you? You act like we're strangers."

"I'm sorry, Briah, I've been going through so much."

"And, I'm your best friend, who's always there." She said.

"I know how things with you are?" I asked, trying not to be the topic of our discussion.

"So much has happened." She said, as she begin telling me about her meeting with Quan and him wanting to be in Chance's life.

"I am so happy for you guys. Chance needs his dad."

"Sure do. I think that Quan is really going to try this time." she said.

"I hope so." I replied.

"I saw Melo." Briah said, causing my heart to get heavy, and I felt the urge to throw up. I ran to the bathroom and threw up.

"Kayla, are you okay?" Briah asked, concerned, standing in the doorway.

"I guess it's something I ate."

"Your ass better take a pregnancy test." she said, joking.

The thought of being pregnant by Derrick caused me to throw up more. Once I was done, I cleaned up and met Briah back in the living room. We caught up with each other, and I got to hang out with my god son. I enjoyed moments like that; when I actually felt like the old Kay. When Briah and Chance left, I decided to go get a pregnancy test. I was so nervous about the results, because with Derrick, there wasn't any telling what could happen. I picked up the test and drank a bottle of water to calm my nerves and help me pee.

When I got home, everything seemed to be moving fast. I had to use the bathroom right away, so I went into the bathroom and peed on the stick. I left the stick on the sink, drank some Nyquil, and laid down on the couch, until I fell asleep.

"Bitch, are you crazy" I heard Derrick yell, kicking me in the stomach. My stomach, instantly, begin to cramp up.

"What did I do?" I cried.

"I saw that test. I know you fucking that nigga, Melo. I'll kill you before you have his baby."

I was terrified, because I knew he would kill me.

"Derrick, please stop." I pleaded, as he dragged me off the couch and begin punching me in my face.

"You're a stupid bitch. You're the reason I am doing this." He cried.

I blocked his blows to my face, causing him to begin punching and kicking me in my stomach, and I could feel something leaking down my leg, as my stomach begin

61

cramping. I knew I was losing this baby, and in a sick, twisted way, I knew that that baby didn't deserve to be born in this madness. I was going in and out of it, as Derrick was giving me the worst beating I had ever endured.

Briah

Quan had been coming around a lot lately, but I wasn't complaining, because Chance needed his father. Chance and Quan bonded like no other. He was at my house, chilling with Chance, so I decided to make us dinner and eat as a family. I was in a good mood, so I made a big feast of fried chicken, macaroni and cheese, collard greens, potato salad, and candied yams.

Quan had Chance outside trying to teach him how to ride a bike, without his training wheels. I went to the back yard and called them in for dinner.

"It smells good as hell in here." Quan said, smiling.

"Thanks, and Quan please stop having my baby riding without his training wheels." I told him.

"Listen, that little nigga isn't going be my seed running around like a little bitch."

"First off, we're not going to refer to him as a little nigga." I said, rolling my eyes.

"You right, Bri." Quan took Chance to wash his hands, and I decided to make their plates.

I fixed both of us drinks, since we both loved Hennessey. They said Hennessey made you crazy, and I wasn't sure if me and Quan should have been drinking, because we were both crazy, as hell. The boys came back into the dining room, and we said grace.

"I can't even lie, Briah, this shit look and smell good." He said, picking up his fork and beginning to eat.

"Thank you." I said, happy he would enjoy it.

"Briah, you still trying to come to Jersey, right?" he asked.

"Yup, your grandmother not going to curse me out." I said, laughing.

"You know she loves you. It's crazy when I was telling her about Chance. She remembered you right away." He said

"Well, I am unforgettable." I said, joking.

"You're right about that."

"So, what the hell is up with you?" I asked.

"Man, these last three years been crazy." He told me.

"You know I needed you." I confessed.

"I know, but you're a strong ass women, who managed to hold it down. Trust and believe, you were better off without me in your life."

"How can you say that?" I asked.

"Trust me, Bri. You're a ride or die chick. All the shit I was into would've consumed your life, and I couldn't do that to you."

"I guess."

"Look at the life you've built for our son, already. I promise that, from this day forward, he will have a different life than the ones we had."

"Hell, yeah. That's why I am working my ass off." My phone rang, interrupting our conversation.

"My bad. Let me get this. I don't know this number.

"Hello." I answered, confused.

"Hi, I have a Kayla Monroe here at Atlanta Medical Center." Said, the person.

"Is she okay?" I cried, causing Quan to look at me with worry.

"Ma'am, can you please come down. We found your contact information in her cell phone." The women said, hanging up.

"You good?" Quan asked.

"Kayla is in the hospital."

"What happened?" he asked.

"I am not sure, but we was just there earlier. Can you please keep Chance, while I go see about her?" I asked.

"Man, go ahead with that. You know, damn well, I got you. Let me know how she's doing." He said.

I got dressed and rushed to the hospital, immediately. I called Kayla's parents, and they told me that they were on the next flight there. I walked through the hospital, nervously. I walked to the nurse's station.

"Hi, someone called me about my friend, Kayla Monroe." I told her, scared.

"Give me one second." The nurse said, as she begin entering Kayla's name in the system.

"I need your ID." She told me.

I handed her my ID and, anxiously, waited to get Kay's room number.

"She's in Room 420." She told me.

I took my pass and raced to Kayla's room. When I got there, she was bruised badly, and it looked like she had been attacked.

Jade

When the cops barged into my house, I just starred at the wall. They were talking to me, but it was like I was in another world. Some went upstairs, and a women cop sat next to me and began to talk, but I didn't have the urge to open my mouth. A cop walked downstairs, shaking his head, and when he looked at me, I saw sympathy in his eyes. I didn't need his sympathy, because I knew I was going to spend the rest of my life in jail.

At 22, my life was ending before it even began.

"Ma'am, can you tell us what happened?" the officer asked.

I just stared at him, with a blank expression, because I didn't feel the need to answer. The female cop that was sitting next to me became annoyed with my silence.

"Can you tell us your name?" She shouted.

"Jade Graham." I told her.

"Well, Jade Graham, you're coming to the station with us." The cop said.

I stood up and followed them. I didn't feel like fighting, especially, when I was guilty. We drove to the station, and I already knew my outcome was going be bad. The situation at hand didn't look too good. I regretted coming back to Atlanta. Every time I was there, something would happen. I was abused by Kenny, hooked on drugs, and I married and undercover gay man.

When we got to the station, they put me in a dark room, where the light was blinking on and off. Two detectives came in, I guess they were going to play the good and bad cop routine that I had saw on cop shows. The first detective was a Hispanic woman, who was in her mid-30's, and she favored the woman, who played Angela, on Power. The second detective was a white man, in his early 40's, and he had salt and pepper hair, with sky blue eyes. He had on a tailored suit that I knew he couldn't afford on a detective's salary.

"Jade, I am Detective Ramos, and this is my partner, Detective Reid." She said, introducing us. I didn't say anything to neither of them. "Jade, can you tell us what happened?" Detective Ramos asked.

I looked at her and shrugged my shoulders. "Look, we know you're the one who did it. Your fancy model career is over. Just tell us what happened, so we can charge you." Detective Reid shouted. Deep down, he was scaring me, but I refused to let him see me sweat. We were interrupted by a knock on the door. I was shocked to see Briah's older boo, 3T.

"Good evening. I am representing Jade Graham." He said, walking in with confidence.

Detective Reid rolled his eyes, and Detective Ramos looked at him with lust in her eyes.

"Can I speak to my client alone?" He asked.

Both Detectives walked out, leaving us alone. I trusted 3T, because I knew Briah sent him.

"Jade, what's going on?" He asked.

I explained to him what had happened, and a smile crept across his face.

"Why are you smiling?" I asked, nervously.

"Because you're going to plead, temporary insanity. We're going to get you out of this mess." he said, with a smile.

"Are you sure?" I asked, confused.

"Yes, my track record is impeccable. The only thing is that the other guy you killed is the mayor's son, so they're going to try to hush you and get you to plea, but we're taking this straight to trial. Sit tight, I need them to place you under arrest, so we can get a bail hearing." He told me, and he left out.

I kind of felt at ease with 3 has my lawyer. I knew that he was expensive, and that I would probably have to sell my condo. I could kiss my career goodbye, because I knew that Scott wasn't going deal with any of my drama. Seconds later, 3 came back with another woman.

"Jade, I am Lindsey Parish, the DA on this case. I want to offer you a plea deal." She said.

"Lindsey, you and I both know that my client still hasn't been charged." 3 said.

She rolled her eyes and walked out. "I am sure that they're putting their asses together to figure out what to charge you with." 3 said, laughing.

Detective Ramos walked into the room with handcuffs.

"Jade Graham, you are under arrest for the murders of Jared Robinson and Darren Pullings." She said, as she begin reading my rights.

When she was done, 3 looked at me, "Jade, they're going process you, and tomorrow, you'll get your bond hearing." He told me.

I nodded my head that I understood, and he left. They took forever to process me, but after they were done, they put me in a cell alone. I was thankful, too, because I had saw jail movies, and I wasn't a fighter. I laid on the uncomfortable cot, stared at the ceiling, and prayed to God that things worked out for me.

The next morning, I was awakened by the guard, sliding me a breakfast tray. The food, alone, made me want to throw up. I refused to eat it, so I sat on my cot and waited for my name to be called for court. An hour later, I was called and transported to court. Even though I was in jail for only twelve hours, fresh air felt good. I walked into the courtroom and felt chills down my arms.

Seeing 3 eased some of my nerves, "Hey, Jade, how are you?" He asked.

"As good as I could be." I told him. My name was called, and we stood in front of the judge. He was an older black male, who looked very scary.

"I am Judge Carlson, and I'll be presiding over People vs. Jade Graham." He said, staring me in the eyes.

"Your honor, I am requesting that bail be denied. The defendant has ties overseas and is a flight risk." The DA said.

"Your honor, my client is a successful, and well-known model. She wants to clear her name and get back to her life." 3T said, defending me.

"I am going to grant bail, until trial. Bail is set at one million dollars, and you will be required to wear an ankle bracelet." He said, hitting his gravel.

I was happy and sad. I knew that I didn't have a million dollars in cash, nor assets.

"Jade, sit tight. I am going to bail you out." 3T said.

"My eyes grew wide. I don't have that kind of money." I whispered.

"It's already done, as long as you don't run away, we're good."

"I have no plans."

I was transported back to the jail, anxiously, waiting for my bail to be posted. My bail was posted in less than an hour, and I couldn't wait to get home to shower. I, then, thought about home and realized I didn't have one. I couldn't go back to my old house. Well, I didn't want to go back there. I walked out of the jail and was surprised to see Scott.

"Hey, Scott." I said.

"Hey, Jade. I would hug you, but you probably didn't wash." He joked.

"I'm surprised you're here." I said.

"You're my friend, and I am here for you, at every step of the way." He said smiling.

Kayla

I woke up in the hospital in a lot of pain, and I noticed Briah balled up in the chair, asleep. I buzzed the nurse, because I was thirsty.

"Welcome back, sleepy head." The nurse said, smiling.

"Can I have water?" I asked. She poured me some water, and I drank it so fast that it gave me a brain freeze. The doctor walked in, and I remembered him from the last time I was there from losing my baby.

"Kayla, I am glad you're up. Do you remember anything?" he asked.

"I remember being attacked by a group of people." I said, lying. I was too scared to tell the truth.

"Well, you were twelve weeks pregnant, but unfortunately, you suffered a miscarriage. You also fractured your skull, and your ankle is sprained. I want to keep you here, at least, for a few days to monitor you." He said, with empathy.

I was actually happy that I had lost the baby, because Lord knows, that having a baby with Derrick was out of the question.

"Kayla, what happened?" Briah said, getting up.

"I was attacked." I told her.

"By who?" she asked, suspiciously.

When I had the urge to tell her what had happened, Derrick walked in.

"Babe, are you okay?" he said, walking over and kissing me. It took everything in me not to spit on him.

"I'll be okay." I said.

"Hey, Briah." Derrick said.

"Hey." Briah said, dryly.

I was nervous that he would suspect that I told them anything.

"I have to go get Chance, but I'll be back, tomorrow. I promise." She said, hugging me.

"It's okay, Briah. I'll take care of her."

"I know, but she's my best friend, so I'll be back." She said, snapping at Derrick and leaving.

Once she left, Derrick turned to me with rage in his eyes. "You told that bitch what happened?"

"Of course not." I said, scared.

My parents walked in, saving me from Derrick.

"Kayla, we came as soon as we got the call. How are you feeling?" My mother asked.

"I am okay. I lost my baby." I said, trying to hold back my tears.

"It's okay, Pumpkin. We're here, now." My dad said, rubbing my head.

"What kind of monster would do this?" My mother said.

"I don't know. I was attacked." I cried, staring at Derrick.

"Don't worry, mom and pops, I'll take care of our baby girl." Derrick said, smiling. I wanted to wipe that bullshit smile off his face.

Briah

A month later...

Quan's grandmother had requested us almost two months ago, but I refused to leave, both Kay, and Jade alone, while they were going through their shit. I thought we were going to drive up there, because we did last time, but Quan got us plane tickets. He said that he wasn't sure how Chance was going to do with a thirteen hour drive. Our flight was cool; I caught up on some reading, while Quan entertained Chance. He fell right into the father role with Chance, and he hadn't even asked for a DNA test, yet, which I was surprised about, because I knew how up and down Quan could be.

Once we landed, Quan's cousin, Nook, was waiting for us.

"Cuddy." Nook shouted, dapping Quan, and staring at me with lust in his eyes.

"Nook, have some damn respect for my baby mama." Quan joked.

"Damn, Cut, you went to the ATL and got you a thick bitch."

"Who you calling a bitch?" I snapped. We hadn't even been here for two hours, and I was already annoyed.

"Nook, chill." Quan said, opening the car door for me and Chance to get in.

The ride was quiet; Quan was focused on his phone, and Nook was stealing glances of me in the mirror, while Chance was sleeping on my lap. We arrived to Quan's grandmother's house, and I was excited. The last time that I met her, she was so warm with me, and her house felt so comfortable. When Quan suggested that we stay there, I did, because I preferred to stay at her place rather than a hotel.

We walked into the house, and the aroma of food filled my nostrils.

"Quannie, is that you?" His grandmother asked, walking into the living room.

She was exactly how I remembered. Hips for days, brown skin, with big brown eyes. Her dread locks were neat and in a bun. She had on a pair of tights, a long shirt that covered her butt, and some sandals on her feet.

"Hey, Ma." Quan said, smiling.

Their relationship was so loving. You could tell that Quan loved his grandmother and that she loved him.

"Come here, little girl, and give grandma a hug." She said, smiling at me. I hugged her and felt the warm feeling of having a motherly figure. "Now, f y'all two, where is that handsome baby?" She said. Chance was hiding behind me.

"Chance, don't hide. This is your grandma." I told him. He took one look at her and ran right to her.

"Yup, this baby is a Harris. Now, y'all go wash up, so you guys can eat." She told us.

We all went to wash our hands and went into the dining room. Quan's grandmother had chicken, rice, cabbage, macaroni and cheese, and sweet potatoes on the table. We sat down, said grace, and begin fixing our plates.

"I gave y'all a month, and you just made it?" She joked.

"My friends have been in some trouble. I couldn't leave them." I told her.

"I hear that, boo, you have loyalty. Quannie, I told you three years ago that this one was a keeper." She said, winking at me.

"Listen, Grandma, right now, I am getting to know my son."

"I wish I could've gotten to know him more." She said, looking at me.

"I'm sorry. When I found out that I was pregnant, Quan was MIA, and then, when I gave birth, he stormed out the hospital." I told her.

"Quannie, I done told you about that temper."

"I am getting better; I'm working on myself, especially, for my son." He said, proudly.

"I am so proud of you, baby." She said, smiling.

"Yeah, I could never be a deadbeat like my punk ass daddy." He said, causing me to choke on my juice. I was praying that he didn't catch it.

"Anyway, I know it's summer, so I want Chance to stay with me until school starts," his grandmother said.

"I only packed enough for a few days."

"Chile, hush, you know damn well I brought that baby some clothes." She said.

I thought about it, and I trusted Quan's grandmother. Not to mention, she missed out on the first two years of his life, and it was so much going on back home.

"Okay, but I am coming to get my baby in a few weeks." I told her.

"No, you're not. I'll be in Georgia. Time to visit there."

"Well, I hate to be rude, but I wanna show my son off to my niggas. We'll be back." Quan said, getting up and grabbing Chance to leave.

"Just like niggas to eat and not clean up." His grandmother fussed.

"I'll help you." I told her.

"I know." She said, laughing.

"Briah, when Quan mentioned his father, I saw you tense up. What's up?" She asked.

"I know who his father is." I confessed.

"How? Does Quannie know?" She asked.

"No, I stumbled upon the news, literally. Black is married to my best friend, L."

"I wish Black would just leave him alone."

"So, you know too?" I asked, confused.

"Yes, girl, I always knew Black killed my daughter's spirit. He was never allowed to be around my Quannie."

"You don't think Quan is going be pissed when he finds out?" I asked.

"How would he know?" She asked.

"Black is trying to get in touch with him, and I have a feeling that they are going to cross paths."

"Oh, boy, Black needs to stay his ass away." She said, rubbing her temple.

"Why didn't you stop Quan from going to Georgia?" I asked, wondering.

"You and I both know that we can't stop Quan from doing shit." She said, laughing.

"I know. I think that his being around Chance has him wanting to know his dad. He mentions him often." I told her.

"Man, fuck Black's ass. He got my daughter into drugs, and he's still a dope dealer." She vented.

"I know, I worked for him for a while." I confessed.

"Seriously, Quan know?"

"Yes." I told her, replaying the entire story of me and Quan's last time having sex, and the night Chance was conceived.

"Well, I know how Quannie gets, so now, it makes sense." She said.

Quan's grandmother and I chilled, until the boys got back. I knew that I was going to enjoy being around her, because she gave me that motherly love.

Jade

Since I had been out on bail, I stayed at Briah's. I didn't feel comfortable going back to the house that I shared with Jared. Scott stayed with me for a few weeks, and then, he had to leave, and my career was put on hold, until the trial was over. 3T worked, day and night, on my case, and I had made the headlines, but a lot of people looked at me with compassion. I was a woman who came home to find her husband in bed with another man.

3T had already told me that all of my skeletons were going to come out, so I was preparing myself. Since I wasn't working, I decided to put my energy into writing a book about my life. People didn't realize how hard it really was to be molested, and then, feel neglected. My mother hadn't reached out to me, but my dad and Ricky did. My father promised me that he would be there for me when the trial started, but I didn't expect my mother to be there for me, at all.

I had to take a lot of physical evaluations and was diagnosed with bipolar. Ricky said that my mother had it, but never admitted to it. I felt played by Jared, because he had me move down here to be closer to his gay lover, and then, married me as a cover up. I was, definitely, ignorant to the gay lifestyle, because in my eyes, Jared didn't fit the gay profile. Then again, what was the profile. I began writing my book and started with my upbringing. I begin shedding tears, thinking about how good things were, before I was molested. My mother was this fun mother that I would go do girl things with, while my dad would do guy stuff with Ricky. The day I lost my innocence, everything changed.

Kayla

My parents stayed with me for a week, and I was, honestly, scared for them to leave. Derrick had been a true gentlemen, while they were there, but I knew that that wasn't going last. I hugged both my parents, tightly, as they boarded their plane. When I got back to the car, Derrick was engrossed in his phone, and I didn't even bother to bother him, because I didn't have any intentions on even talking to him.

"You going to that bullshit job, tomorrow?" He spat.

"Yes, Derrick, you know I love my job." I told him, rolling my eyes.

"You love your job or being around that nigga, Melo." He said.

"I don't even see Melo, nor talk to him. You're crazy." I said, rolling my eyes, again.

I should have never said that, because Derrick hauled off and punched me on the side of my face. I was barely healed from two weeks ago, and I was sure that this wound would be fresh. I was so sick and tired of being abused. The rest of the car ride was quiet. Derrick dropped me off and kept going, and I didn't mind, because I, honestly, didn't want to be near him. Once I got home, I put an ice pack on my face and relaxed. We kept those in the house for obvious reasons. I cried myself to sleep, because I felt so alone and didn't feel like I had anything to live for, anymore.

The next morning, I got up to get ready for work. I chose a pair of pink Pixie pants, a white collared shirt, and some Gucci flats. When I looked in the mirror, I couldn't believe my face was swollen, again. I put on as much make-up as I could to conceal it, because I had to go to work. I wore my hair down to try and hide the bruises, too. I wasn't in the best mood when I got to work, because I was so embarrassed. I arrived extra early, because I knew that substitutes didn't necessarily take care of the classrooms. As I was cleaning, Principal Greene walked in.

"Well, hello, missy. Just seeing how you're doing." She said, with a smile.

"I am doing okay." I told her.

"Are you sure?" She asked, raising her eyebrow.

"Yes." I snapped.

"Whoa, relax." she said, looking offended.

"I am so sorry. I am under a lot of stress." I explained.

"I understand. Maybe you should take more time off." She told me.

"No, I need to get out of that house." I explained.

"Well, Kayla, I see that you're on edge, not to mention, your eye is swollen. I can't have you around the kids or parents like that." I could feel the tears form in my eyes. "Don't cry, baby. Look, on a personal level, I am here for you, and I think that you're a beautiful person and an awesome teacher, but you need to work on yourself." She said, kissing me on my forehead and leaving.

I gathered my things, while hiding my tears. Once I got in my car, I replayed all the times Derrick whooped my ass and all the times he made me feel like nothing. I started my car and drove straight into the pole in front of me hoping that God would've numbed the pain and praying that I was dead.

Carmelo

I was dropping off Cameron when I saw Kayla run out of the school in tears. I had been worried about little mama, especially, when I heard she was in the hospital, because I knew that that whack ass nigga was beating her ass. I didn't know that Kayla, because the Kayla I was with would have put a nigga in their place and kept it moving.

"Daddy, I have two girlfriends." Cam said, skipping to school. I shook my head. He should have been my nigga, Quan's son, 'cause that's how Quan sounded.

"Well, little man, eventually you're going to find the one who will make you a one woman man." I told him, laughing.

We heard a loud crashing noise, causing both of us to turn around. I noticed that Kayla's car was wrapped around the pole and on fire. My first instinct was to run over there.

"Cam, please go inside and get an adult." I said, running before he could respond.

Seeing the love of my life car wrapped around a pole ate me up. I got there and she wasn't in the car; she was thrown into the grass. People were starting to come outside.

"I called the police." The principal said, running towards me.

I found Kay, sprawled in the grass, unconscious. Tears begin roll down my face, as I thought about losing her.

Briah

My trip to Jersey with Quan was good. We were in a good place. I was happy when Quan's grandmother offered to keep Chance. Between Jade and Kayla, those heifer's was going to cause me to lose my mind. Lauren had been texting me, nonstop, about getting Quan over to the house, but I wanted no parts of it. Quan and I were doing good, and I knew, that if he found out that I knew Black was his father, he wouldn't speak to me. Lauren and I were doing our ritual today of hitting up the spa. I prayed that she kept things short and sweet and didn't bring up Quan.

When I arrived at the spa, Lauren was sitting in the pedicure seat, sipping champagne.

"Hey, boo. You look good." She said, smiling.

"Thanks, you always look good." I told her, taking a seat.

"So, what's new, heffa?" She asked.

"Well, I just got back from Jersey, and we let Chance meet his grandmother." I told her.

"That's good. He does have a grandpa, too." She said.

"Look, I get it, but honestly, that is something between Black and Laquan, and I don't even feel comfortable talking about this. It's bad enough that his grandmother and I were discussing it."

"Wait, that bitch knew, too. That family is so damn shiesty." She snapped.

"Don't talk about her like that." I said, defending her.

"Well, I feel like they're over there trying to keep my husband away from his son."

"For one, Quan is damn near 30, Black need to stop calling him and just chase him down so that he can tell him."

"Black said that, maybe we can have dinner at the house, and you bring Quan."

"Nope, I am not getting involved, and I don't want to talk about this shit, anymore." I snapped.

"Damn, Briah. I am just trying to be there for my husband."

"And, I am trying to build a strong relationship with my son's father." I said, drying my feet off and walking out.

Lauren and Black was really starting to piss me off. I left the spa and went back to work. When I got there, 3 and his friend from last time were in the office in an embrace.

"Hey, Briah. You remember Jackie?" he said, introducing us.

"I do. Nice to see you, again." I told her, faking my smile.

"Well you will be seeing a lot of her." he said, smiling showing me her ring finger. The day couldn't get any worst.

"Congratulations." I said, holding up a fake smile.

"Baby, I have to go. Briah, nice seeing you, again." She said, looking at me and leaving.

"So, how was the Jersey trip?" he asked.

"It went good. Chance is still there bonding with his paternal grandmother."

"Is it safe over there?" he asked.

"Of course, why wouldn't it be?" I said, becoming annoyed.

"Just saying."

"What are you trying to say?" I asked, confused.

"I hope his father doesn't come in and out of his life."

"Listen 3, I respect you, and I am a hundred and ten percent grateful for everything you have done, but when it comes to Quan and Chance, that's my business."

"Well, I am just looking out for you."

"You should be looking out for yourself." I snapped.

"What you trying to say?" He asked.

"All I am saying is Jackie seems really happy."

"She's not like that."

"You know what, good luck with it. Right now, I am going to leave, so worse things aren't said." I told him.

I left the office and tried to gather my emotions. I thought I was really lusting for 3T, but maybe, I wasn't. Maybe I was looking for a positive male figure in my life. That was something I had never gotten. My brothers were good to me, but they weren't living positive. I often wondered how they were doing, and I knew that they would be coming home one day. Hopefully, we could all reunite. My phone began to ring, knocking me out of my thoughts. I didn't recognize the number, so of course, I was leery about answering.

"Hello." I answered.

"Briah, this Melo I need you to come to the hospital ASAP. It's about Kay." he said, sounding scared.

I was nervous as fuck. Kayla just got out of the hospital. I, definitely, needed to pay more attention to what was going on with her. I rushed straight to the hospital, and when I got there, Melo was sitting in a chair, covering his face.

"Mel?" I said, nervously.

I noticed that he had tears in his eyes, and I had never seen Melo cry.

"Yo', B, Kayla not doing good at all." He said, shaking his head.

"What happened?" I asked, as I felt my heart beating outside of my chest.

"She hit a pole. They were saying that she did it on purpose."

"Nah, Kay, loved life. She wouldn't try and kill herself."

"Listen, Kay ain't been right in a minute. Remember when I told you to keep an eye on her?" he said.

"Yeah, but I thought you were overreacting."

"Why would I? My son is in her class, and she would come in with bruises and shit. Even her boss told her take time off."

"I knew it was something about Derrick that rubbed me the wrong way." I said, thinking about the times when he was acting nutty.

"Man, that nigga is mad possessive."

"Briah, what happened to Kayla?" Derrick asked, walking in.

"Nigga, you better take those two feet and walk the fuck out of here." Melo warned him.

"I ain't going nowhere. This my girl."

"Derrick, have you been putting your hands on Kay?" I said, standing up.

"I don't know what she told you, but that was accident." He confessed.

Melo and I looked at each other, confused, because neither one of us mentioned a particular time.

"What was an accident?" Before I could finish talking, Melo punched him in his face.

"Mel, stop!" I shouted. As much as I wanted to see Derrick get his ass whooped, I didn't want Melo in jail or kicked out. Derrick flinched and walked off before security came.

"Mel, you good?" I asked.

"Yeah, I just can't control it with him. I'mma kill that nigga." Mel said, with venom in his voice.

While we waited for Kayla to get out of surgery, I called her parents, and of course, they were frantic, because she had just got out of the hospital. They said that they were on their way.

"Family of Kayla Monroe." The doctor said, walking up to us.

"Right here." I said, as we both stood up.

"Your friend suffered a broken collar bone. She also had a lot of swelling in her brain, so we had to put her in an induced coma. Right now, we're just trying to keep her comfortable." He said and then left.

"I don't get what the hell is going on." I said, confused.

"Man, that nigga Derrick gone get it." Melo said.

"What if she doesn't wake up, Mel?" I cried."

"She will, B, don't worry." He said, giving me a hug.

I felt like a bad friend; it was like I had failed her. I had so many other things going on that I didn't pay attention to the signs.

Jade

My palms were sweating, because it was the first day of my trial, and I was nervous. 3T was good at what he did, but I was still very scared. As promised, my dad was there, and I couldn't have been more grateful. My dad, Ricky, and Scott were super supportive.

"Jade, are you ready?" 3T asked.

"More than I would like to be." I told him.

We got out of the car and walked into the courtroom, with cameras flashing from all angles. My case had become a spectacle. I had become a household name, but not the way I preferred. It was like people were obsessed with my case. I took a seat at the table and looked around, where I saw my dad, Ricky, and Scott, but I didn't see Briah. Since everything had happened, she and I had gotten really close.

I knew that she had a lot to deal with Kayla being in a coma, so I prayed that things got better for all of us. It was like we couldn't catch a break. I sat and stared into space, as the prosecutor did her opening statement. It was all a bunch of bullshit. She tried to paint me as this crazed, drug addicted model, who killed her husband and lover in a drunken rage, when that was farthest from the truth. The prosecutor had a weak case. Her only witness was the police who came, when I killed Jared and his lover. I watched the cop tell the prosecutor how I wouldn't say anything and just stared into space, as they were trying to figure out what happened. I had a little hope that this would help my temporary insanity plea. The prosecutor was upset that I wouldn't take a plea deal, because they didn't want the mayor's secret to get out, but I didn't care. 3T said I had a fighting chance, and I was going take it.

Briah

Lauren was helping me cook, when the doorbell rang. It was Quan's grandmother, Dolores, and Chance. I went to get the door, and Chance ran straight to me.

"Mama!" He said, in his little voice, running towards me. I picked him up and held him in my arms. I missed my son.

"Well, I guess I am nobody." Dolores said, with her hand on her hip.

"Now, you know I love you, Ma. I just missed my baby." I said, putting Quan down and giving her a hug.

"Well, it smells good in here. Let me find out you cooking." She said.

"I am trying to be like you. I wanted to cook you a special dinner." I told her.

"Well, heffa, if you can't cook, you know I am going to tell you, and who is this Barbie doll?" She said, looking at Lauren.

"Oh, that's my friend, Lauren. Lauren, this is Quan's Grandmother, Dolores." I introduced.

"Nice to meet you, pretty girl. I can tell you got a rich nigga taking care of you." She said, laughing. I wanted to say you have no idea.

"Well, Bri, I have to go home and cook for my rich nigga." Lauren said, laughing.

"Why don't you bring your man over here for dinner, shit, I need a rich man. He got friends?" Dolores said.

I was shaking my head, but she didn't get the memo.

"That's a good idea. Bri said dinner would be ready by 6:30. See you guys then." She said, grabbing her bag and running out.

She knew I was going say something, which is why she ran out like that.

"Ma, you have no idea what you just did." I told her.

"What you mean?" She asked

"That's Quan's father, Black, fiancé," I told her.

"Well, call that heffa, and tell her don't come."

"She's not going to listen. She's been begging me to make Quan meet up with Black, but I didn't want anything to do with it."

"Quan is going flip out." She said.

"Sure is. Maybe they won't say anything." I prayed.

Dolores helped me with dinner, and I told her to let me finish, but she couldn't help it. It was almost 6:30, and Quan had come a little early, but he was with Chance, keeping him company. Jade didn't know anything about cooking, so she just set the table. The doorbell rang, and I looked at Dolores.

"Answer it. I ain't scared of that nigga." Dolores said.

I opened the door, and Lauren and Black walked in with all smiles.

"Hey, y'all." I said, letting them in just as Quan and Chance walked into the dining room.

"Black, what you doing here?" Quan asked.

"My shawty told me your grand mom's invited us for dinner."

"Nah, we ain't offer that." Quan said.

I grabbed Lauren's arm and whispered.

"Now, why would you come? I told you that I didn't want any parts of this paternity bullshit."

"Well, I think Quan should know." Lauren said, yanking her arm away from me.

Dolores walked in and looked at Black with a smug look.

"Well, if it ain't Lady D. Long time, no see." Black said, smirking.

"Leave me alone, black ass." She said, rolling her eyes.

"Ma, you know this nigga?" Quan asked. My heart begin beating fast.

"Of course she does; isn't that right?" Black said.

"Whatever." She said.

"Somebody better tell me something. I ain't with that fufu shit!" Quan yelled, causing Chance to start crying.

I was guessing that he didn't like to see his father upset, and honestly, I didn't like to see it either.

"Why don't we just all sit down and talk." Lauren said, trying to diffuse everything.

"Nope, too late for all that, little Ms. Barbie. Look Quan, Black is your father." Dolores finally told him.

"What type of family bullshit is that? Man, fuck y'all. I'm out!" Quan said, leaving.

"Quan, don't do this. You don't need to be alone." I pleaded.

"Nah, I need to get away from all y'all untrustworthy motherfuckers. Who knew about this?" He shouted, as he slammed the door.

"I knew that this was going happen." I said, getting mad at Lauren.

"Well, it was bound to happen. Quan needed to know the truth." Lauren said.

"Look, L, you and Black should leave." I told them.

"Quan shouldn't be mad at no one, but Dolores. She's the one that kept him away from me."

"And, I don't regret it, especially, the way you did my Katie."

"Man, Katie had been fucked up, before I met her. I'm out." Black said, leaving with Lauren following behind.

"I wish I could say he'll come around, but we both know how stubborn his ass is." Dolores said.

"Exactly. I just wanted my son to have relationship with his father, but now, I am not sure."

"Don't worry. Look, I am going to eat. You worked so hard on this food." She said, kissing me on my forehead.

I hoped that she was right, but I knew that, once Quan pushed you away, there was no telling when he would allow you back into his life.

Kayla

Wherever I was, it was an amazing feeling. It felt like an outer body experience. Two little girls were close by, but I couldn't touch them. One looked exactly like Melo, and she had a certain twinkle in her eye. I couldn't make out how the other girl looked, but she had a different look in her eyes. I could also hear Melo, Kayla, and my parent's voices. I wanted to reach out and speak, but I couldn't. I also wondered where Derrick was.

"Mama." One of the little girls said.

I walked over to them, but I couldn't touch them. The little girl, who I assumed was mines and Melo's, dropped a flower, grabbed the other girl, and ran away. I tried to chase them, but I couldn't. I gathered all of my strength, and I opened my eyes. When I opened them, Carmelo was standing there, smiling.

"Kayla." He said, smiling.

I couldn't talk, because I was hoarse, and my body ached. The nurse walked in and brought me some water, and I got a brain freeze, again.

"Ouch." I said.

"Are you okay?" Melo asked, nervously.

"Yes, Mel, I am fine. I had a brain freeze." I said, smiling.

"Kayla, the doctor will be in shortly." The nurse said, with a smile, while sneaking a glance over at Mel. I wondered if she thought he was my man.

"Kayla, you remember anything?" He asked.

"Yes, I remembering everything" I told him.

"I'mma kill that nigga Derrick!" He shouted.

"Why?" I asked.

"You still defending that nigga?" He said, with a look of disgust.

'Mel, what nigga? I don't know who Derrick is." I said, confused.

"You said you remembered everything."

"Umm, yeah. The accident when I was driving home from the doctor. Oh yeah, it's a girl." I said, smiling and rubbing my flat stomach.

"Wait, what happened to our baby?" I said, getting scared. The look on Mel's face scared me.

"Kay, what year is it?" He asked.

"Umm, it's 2013." I told him, matter-of-factly. The doctor came in smiling.

"Kayla, I am glad you're awake. We have some things to discuss." He said.

"Umm, Doc, we need to talk." Mel said.

"I have to do an examination first." The doctor said.

"Kayla what year is, again?" Melo asked.

"For the last time, 2013." She said, rolling her eyes. The doctor looked at Mel with concern, and I was confused.

"Kayla, its 2015." The doctor said, confusing me.

How could I forget the last two years of my life? When my parents walked, in I knew something wasn't right.

Jade

While the trial was going on, I continued to write my book about my life. I prayed that, one day, my struggles could help the next person. I was working on my book when 3 called me. My heart was beating fast, and I was scared of the news he was going to deliver.

"Hello." I said, picking up the phone.

"Hey, Jade. I have some new developments."

"What is it?" I asked, nervously.

"The prosecutor realized that she's going to lose the case. It's clear that the murder wasn't planned, and any person could've killed their brand new husband and lover in a state of confusion." He explained.

"Okay, so that's it?" I asked, still confused.

"Not exactly. The judge will sign off, but only if you agree to inpatient therapy and counseling."

"Listen, I have already been to rehab and have had a lot of therapy. I am not interested in going down that road, again."

"Well, Jade, it's either that, or continue this trial. And, what if they have a change of heart. I am telling you that it's for the best."

"Well, how long do I have to decide?" I asked.

"Honestly, I wouldn't wait a minute later."

"Well, can I call my brother and pray on it?"

"Yes, Jade, I am calling you back in 30 minutes." He said, hanging up.

Instead of calling Ricky, I drove straight to his house. When I got there, Ricky answered.

"Hey sis, what's so urgent?" he asked.

I walked in and told him what 3T had just told me.

"So, what you think?" I asked.

"I think it's a good idea. You're, basically, getting off easily."

"But, I already did all that." I told him.

"Yeah, because you had an addiction. I think more counseling can do you better than harm."

"You're right. I was writing a book about my life and a lot of old feelings came back." I confessed.

"See what I mean. Write this book, go away for a few months, close all those nasty chapters in your life, and God will bless you." Ricky said.

"Thank you, Ricky, I feel a lot better, now." I said, hugging him.

I called 3 with my answer, and the next day I was going to sign the deal and enter treatment. My dad was staying at Ricky's, so for the rest of the day, I kicked it with them. I just wished my mom and I could get along, because she belonged right next to us.

Briah

Since the drama with Quan finding out about Black being his father, he had barely said anything to me. I wanted to curse his ass out, because I had nothing to do with it, but instead, I chose to be the mature adult. He still came and got Chance, and his grandmother planned to stay a few months. He even refused to talk to her. Lauren told me that he wasn't taking Black's calls, either, but I wasn't surprised. I knew he would never talk to Black, again. It felt good to be back at work. Sometimes, dealing with someone else's drama helped you focus on other things.

I was finishing up paperwork with Jade's case, and I was so happy that she was getting off. I hoped that, once she was out of treatment, things would get better for her. I was typing up paperwork for 3, when I heard heels click clacking. I looked up, and Jackie walked through like an extra from rip the runway.

"Where's 3?" She asked, with attitude.

"Umm, he's in court." I replied.

"I have to talk to him about the way you speak to me." She said.

"Are you serious, 'cause you walked in with an attitude." I told her.

"Whatever, little girl, 3 told me what you said about our engagement, and you better mind your business." She said, sticking her finger in my face.

"Listen, bitch, you won't have a fucking finger." I said, smacking her hand away from my face.

"Ladies." 3T said, walking out of the elevator.

"Hey, baby, I was just asking Briah where you were." Jackie said, putting on a fake voice

"Well, daddy's here now." 3 said, smiling.

I wanted to throw up, but I kept my composure.

"How did everything go?" I asked.

"Everything went fine. Jade is going to treatment and will be back, better than ever."

"That's great." I said.

"Can we get some fresh air, baby, I hate the way it smells in here?" Jackie said, frowning her nose up.

"Like what, I'll talk to the cleaning people."

"It smells like the funky New York streets." She said, smirking at me.

"Oh, baby, please. Let's get out of here. See you later, Briah." He said, waving.

I gave him a fake smile and rolled my eyes at Jackie. It was something about that bitch that I didn't like. I knew just who to hit up about her. I pulled out my phone and called his daughter, Angel. Everybody knew she was a daddy's girl, and he was big on his baby, Angel. The phone rang a few times before she answered.

"Hey, Briah." She answered. Angel had always been cool to me. She had been through hell and back, and she managed to survive and stay humble.

"Hey, boo. How are the kiddies and hubby?" I asked.

"Everybody is fine. The only people getting on our nerves is our mothers." She said, joking.

I had met both of their mothers and knew they were a hot mess. They could, definitely, be in a reality show with Dolores.

"I just have a question, but it's a bit personal." I told her.

"Well, you're like fam, so what is it?" She asked.

"Have you met your father's fiancé?" I asked.

"You know God works in mysterious ways, because I wanted to hit you up and ask you about her, but I wasn't sure if I should."

"Listen, that bitch is faker than a dollar bill, and she has your father wrapped around his finger."

"Well, my grandmother likes her, probably because she's black, and my grandmother is faker than a dollar bill."

Angel joked, causing me to laugh.

"Well, I am going do a little digging on my end." I told her.

"I am, too. Thanks, Briah."

"Of course, your father was there for me when no one was."

"I get it. Don't be trying to be my stepmother." She joked.

"Bye, Angel." I said, laughing.

I knew her name was Jackie Morrison, so the first I thing I did was google her and searched for her on social media, but I came up short. Then, I thought about when I watched a T.V. show where women searched for their husband's mistresses on a dating site. I searched for Jackie on the dating site, and her picture appeared. There were so many comments about her scamming rich older dudes. I smiled on the inside, because this bitch was almost out of my life.

Kayla

When my parents walked in, I was more confused, because they had stopped talking to me a long time ago.

"Kayla, what the hell were you thinking?" My mother said, walking in, being dramatic.

Melo looked like he wanted to say something.

"What are you guys talking about? You don't even talk to me." I said, confused.

"What, what did you do?" My mother shouted, redirecting her attention to Carmelo.

"Ma, don't start blaming him for stuff. He didn't even do anything." I said, defending him.

"I damn sure didn't. I'm out. Feel better, Kay." He said, getting up and leaving.

"Carmelo is my boyfriend. I wish you guys learn to accept him." I cried.

"What about Derrick?" My mother asked.

"Who's Derick?" I asked, in confusion.

A tall guy walked in, carrying balloons and followers, and there was something about him that made me feel weird.

"Derrick, hunny, finally you're here. Kayla is out of her mind."

"Of course I am. The doctor told me that I lost three years of memory." I shouted. My mother was getting on my fucking nerves.

"Damn, baby. I am sure once we get back to our place, you'll have your memory back. We had so many wonderful memories." Derrick said, touching my hand, but I quickly moved my hand away from him.

My mother caught me up on the last three years, and I couldn't believe that I had lost a child, because of Melo or that I was in a relationship with this Derrick person and couldn't remember him. Everything seemed so crazy. I still didn't get what I was doing there. There was something about Derrick that didn't sit right with me, but he seemed to get along with my parents, so I guess I had to give him a chance.

A week later, the doctor cleared me to go home. My home was a home that I didn't remember. Apparently, before the accident, I lived with Derrick. I had to do physical therapy, and the doctor assured me that, with time, my memory should come back. Carmelo had come back to the hospital, but once I found out that I had lost my baby because of him, I kicked him out and told him not to come back. It wasn't like we was together, anyway. Briah was pissed at me and claimed that Carmelo had saved my life, and she had negative things to say about Derrick, but I didn't pay her any mind. Plus, my parents told me Derrick was a good guy.

"You ready, babe?" Derrick asked, walking into the room, smiling.

"Yes." I said, nervously.

I was ready to get out of the hospital, but I wasn't sure about going to Derrick's, because I couldn't remember. Our car ride was quiet. He sang along to the radio, and I was in my own thoughts, wondering what the hell was next for me. I played with my fingers and told myself that I needed to make a nail appointment. My hair looked a mess, and I remembered it being long. Now, it was in a bob that was in a desperate need of a trim and wash. We pulled up to a nice, modest home, but it wasn't as big as the home that I shared with Melo. It was still beautiful, though. We walked in and nothing was familiar about the home. I heard my mother in the kitchen talking.

I knew that this guy, Derrick had to be an Angel if my mother liked him. Not to mention, she was cooking in his kitchen.

"Hey, baby. I made you a feast. Welcome home." She said, kissing me on the cheek.

Derrick and I washed our hands, and when we walked in the dining room, my mouth watered. My mother wasn't lying when she said she made a feast. There was turkey, stuffing, rice & gravy, macaroni & cheese, string beans, and ham. She also baked a cake and made a pie, and she was nice enough to make my plate. I sat down and begin eating like a pig, since I didn't have any real food in the hospital, and I couldn't remember the last time I had my mother's cooking. Dinner was awkward, because my parents and Derrick chatted like they were old friends, and I felt like an outsider.

"Kayla, you know Derrick is a cop?" My dad boasted like he was his son.

"Oh, I didn't know." I said, not really caring.

My parents were team Derrick, so bad, it was actually disgusting.

"Yeah, unlike that thug, Melo." My mother said.

"He is not a thug." I said, defending him.

Derrick looked over at me, and I could see that he didn't like my comment.

"Well, before you guys go back to Texas, I just want to say I love you all like a family, and I am ready to be a part of your family. Kayla, will you marry me?" Derrick asked, holding a ring in his hand.

I looked at how happy my parents were, and it did feel good to have them back in my life.

"Yes." I said, smiling not knowing what the hell I was doing. Not to mention, thoughts of Melo had been running through my mind since I woke up.

But I could make myself love Derrick and get Carmelo out of my system.

Jade

I signed my plea deal, nervously, because I wasn't comfortable with going back into treatment, however, treatment beat a life sentence any day.

"Jade, I hope everything works out for you." 3T said with a smile.

"Thank you. I really appreciate everything you have done for me."

"Of course, anybody that is friends with Briah is good with me. Good luck, Jade." 3T said, giving me a hug.

I walked out of the police station with a sigh of relief. My brother and father were waiting for me to take me to a treatment center outside of Atlanta. I got in the back seat and Ricky drove off.

"Jade, I am proud of you, baby girl." My father said.

"Really, I thought I let everyone down, especially, lately." I said.

"Sis, you have been dealt a lot of bad hands, but I think God is going to put you in another space." Ricky said.

"I sure hope so. I wish mom could have been here." I said, sadly.

"Your mom is dealing with her own issues; you and her are more alike than you guys both realize. Right now, focus on getting better, and when you come back, things will fall into place. I promise." My dad, assured me.

For some reason, I felt hopeful. We pulled up to the Redmond Treatment Center, and it was a beautiful estate, instead of mental facility.

"Good luck, sis. I love you." Ricky said, as I got out the car.

I said my goodbyes to them and walked into the facility. I walked up to the woman sitting at the desk.

"Hi, my name is Jade Graham, and I am here to check in." I told her.

"Okay, give me a second, sugar." She said, with a smile. She typed a few things into the computer and had me sign some paperwork.

"I am going to show you to your room, so you can get settled, and I will need a urine sample." She told me.

She gave me a rundown of what to expect while I was there and that I had a lot of therapy to cover.

"I'll let you get settled. Someone else will get your urine, and then, your doctor will be here to speak with you." She said, closing the door.

My room was small; I had a twin size bed, dresser, and small desk. I was happy that I brought my lap top, because while I was here, I was determined to get my book done.

Briah

"Married." I said, rolling my eyes at Kayla.

"Yes, so are you going to be my maid of honor?" She asked.

I wanted to say hell no, but I had to put the supportive friend role on. "Sure will. When is the date?" I asked.

"Derrick says six months from now."

"That's fast." I told her.

"Well, according to everyone, we been together for two years."

"I guess so. Have you spoken to Melo?" I asked her.

"No, why would I?" she asked, confused.

"Because, he saved your life, Kayla." I told her.

"I still don't understand why I would try to harm myself. You know, more than anyone, how much I love my life and how I wouldn't do anything to ruin this face." she said, joking.

"Yeah, me either." I said.

"Anyway, have you spoken to Jade?" She asked.

"No, she doesn't want to speak to anyone, until she comes out."

"Oh, okay. I feel bad that we never got to get together. My life must has been a mess these past two years." She joked.

"Not that bad. You know you worked as a teacher." I told her.

"No, I didn't. I can't believe no one told me that."

"I am not surprised." I mumbled, as the doorbell rang.

"Let me get that." I said, getting up, wondering who it could be. I answered the door and was shocked to see Melo and Quan standing there.

"Umm, hello." I said.

"Briah, you going to let us in, with your funky ass?"

"Umm, no, nigga. Your ass been ignoring me since that shit with Black went down."

"Look, I am your baby daddy." Quan said, laughing.

"How could I ever forget?" I said, rolling my eyes.

"Where little man at?" Quan asked.

"Maybe, if your ass would speak to your grandmother, you would know that she took him to the movies." I said.

"Yeah, whatever." Quan said, pushing his way in with Melo following.

"Mel?" I said, nervously.

"Carmelo, what are you doing here?" Kayla asked getting up from the couch.

"I came with dickhead over here." He said, pointing to Quan.

"Why you here, Quan?" I asked.

"I can't come see my son, damn, go bring something to drink." Quan ordered.

"I ain't your maid." I snapped.

"Go get me something to drink." he said, snapping his fingers, causing Quan and Kayla to laugh.

"Melo, Kay, y'all want something? I asked.

"Yeah, give me whatever you getting minus the spit I know you going to put in that nigga drink." Melo said, laughing.

"I'll go with you." Kayla said, getting off the couch.

We walked into the kitchen, and I poured three glasses of henny for me, Quan, and Melo. Kayla poured a glass of wine for herself.

"Briah, I am leaving after this glass." Kayla told me.

"Why?" I asked.

"Because Melo is here, and I am not comfortable." She confessed.

"Kay, just chill. Look they both are our exes. Neither one of us are going to get into something crazy." I said, trying to convince myself.

I knew how things went with me and Quan. The guys had turned the game on and was kicking back, chilling.

"I see some people made themselves at home." I said, rolling my eyes.

"Chill, Briah." Melo said, taking his drink out of my hand.

I gave Quan his drink and sat next to him; Kayla sat on the opposite side of Melo. Quan, Melo, and I were into the game, and Kayla was glued to her phone.

"This is, definitely, like old times, with Kay stuck-up ass not trying to mingle with us." Quan joked, causing us to laugh.

"Whatever, Quan, old times would be Briah and I killing y'all in spades." She said, laughing.

"Oh shit. That's what we on? Briah, I know you got some cards." Melo said.

"I sure do. We can get y'all asses real quick." I said, challenging them.

We all got up and made our way to the kitchen table. The rest of the night we got drunk, reminisced, and played cards. It definitely brought me back to the good ole days.

"I am getting tired, and I am tipsy, Briah. I'm going to crash in my old bed." Kayla said, yawning.

"Okay guys. Y'all don't have to go home, but yeah, y'all know the rest." I said, laughing, but I was dead serious.

"It's fine; I got pussy to get home to." Quan said, standing up.

"Goodnight, Briah. Thanks for the hospitality. Gotta do this again, lil' sis." Melo said, hugging me.

Quan saying he had a girl kind of had me feeling some type of way.

"Bye, dirty." Quan said, mushing me.

"So, you got a girlfriend?" I asked, rolling my eyes.

"Little something; nothing serious."

"Yeah, whatever. That bitch better not be around my son." I said, rolling my eyes.

"Like Daddy Warbucks wasn't around him."

"Laquan Harris, get out!" I told him.

"Awe, Briah, you're jealous. I'm out." He said, kissing my cheek.

I quickly moved and went into my room. Kayla and Melo were talking, so I hoped that she saw their asses out. Quan annoyed the fuck out of me.

I was awakened by Chance shaking me, "Mama." He said, smiling.

"Yes, baby." I said, yawning. The smell of food fully woke me up.

Dolores must've cooked, because I knew, damn well, that Kayla didn't. I got up, washed my face, brushed my teeth, and made my way downstairs.

"Good morning." I said to Dolores.

"Morning, boo. I see y'all had a long night, drinking henny and playing cards without me." She joked.

"That's all your grandson." I said, making a plate of bacon, grits, biscuits, and eggs.

"I made a lot of food; I heard y'all nasty asses upstairs." She fussed.

"No you didn't. Quan went home to his girlfriend."

"Chile, please, the only girl he got, is you."

"I don't think so, Ma."

"So, then who the hell was fucking last night?" Dolores said.

Just then, we saw Melo and Kayla walking down the stairs, embarrassed.

"There's your answer." I said, laughing.

Kayla

Derrick's marriage proposal really surprised me. I felt like saying yes was more for him and my parents' than for myself. My mother insisted on staying in Atlanta to help me plan the wedding, and she was driving me crazy, with wedding plans; Derrick was a bit overwhelming when it came to me regaining my memory. I went to see Briah, because honestly, everything with her was genuine, and she was my real friend. We were chilling, and I was surprised that Melo and Quan showed up. Seeing Melo gave me butterflies. It was bad enough that I thought about him all day, but seeing him did something to me. The entire night, I couldn't help but stare at him and wish I was going to our old place, instead of with Derrick. Fooling around with Briah, Quan, and Melo made me think about the old times and all the fun we had.

The guys were getting ready to leave, and I was tired. I made my way to the bottom of Briah's steps, and Melo grabbed my arm.

"Yo', Kay, you good?" He asked, looking concerned.

"Yes, Carmelo." I said, smiling, slurring my words.

"Yeah, whatever. Why you back with fuck boy?"

"Look, I was told that he was my man."

"I am your man." he said, smiling.

"I wish." I mumbled.

"Kayla, I hate games, Ma. You know that this past few months, I watched you be someone you're not." He said, getting closer, causing my body to get a tingling feeling.

"What you know?" I said, smirking.

"That you been wanting this." He said, kissing me.

We stood in the hallway, kissing like two teenagers. I grabbed his hand and guided him upstairs.

"Just lay back, Ma." He said, once we got in the room.

Carmelo begin kissing my neck and his scent filled my nostrils. I wanted that moment forever. Even though I was drunk, I knew my feelings were true. I wish I could just have that moment forever, but I knew that Melo and I would never work.

I woke up the next morning, trying to gather myself, and I looked around and realized that I was in my old room at Briah's house. I looked over, and Melo was looking at me.

"What happened?" I asked.

"I am sure you know what happened, but first, you need to take care of that breath." He joked.

I flipped him the bird and got up to wash my face and brush my teeth. When I got back in the room, Melo was fully dressed.

"Your phone been bugging all morning. I'm surprised you didn't hear it." He said, tossing me my phone.

I looked at my phone, and I had several missed calls from my mother and Derrick.

"Look, Kayla, I'm out. Talk to you later. Let me know if fuck boy, Derrick, do something crazy."

"Why would he?" I asked.

"Nothing." He said, walking downstairs.

I followed him and heard Briah and Dolores talking. I was praying that he could walk out, and I could shower, and go home. Melo waved bye to them and left. I tried to run up the stairs, but I heard Dolores yell my name.

"Not so fast, hot in the ass. I could barely sleep the way y'all was fucking. Bring your ass here." She said. Briah was laughing at her.

"Don't laugh, Briah." I said, rolling my eyes.

"Don't be mad at me miss, I am engaged to another man." She snapped.

"He called me a thousand times. What should I do?" I asked.

"Wash and say you and Briah got drunk and fell asleep." Dolores said.

"Damn, that lie just fell right off your tongue." Briah said.

"I used to be good at my shit back in the day." She bragged.

I ate breakfast and bugged out with Dolores and Briah for a while. I didn't even waste my time calling Derrick. I didn't feel the need to really answer to him, so I would speak with him once I got home.

When I was done hanging out with Briah, I got my stuff together and headed home. My mother and Derrick were in the living room, watching TV.

"Kayla, we were worried sick." My mother said.

"Well, hello to you, too, mother, and I am grown. I texted Derrick and told him where I was."

"Don't get cute, little girl."

"I am grown, last I check." I told my mother.

"That's why I don't like you around Briah. Some of that street edge is rubbing off on you." Derrick said.

"Well, get used to her, because she not going anywhere, and I asked her to be my maid of honor." I told him.

"Whatever, baby. It's your choice. Some things just don't deserve a fight." He said, kissing me on the lips.

"Kayla, I wanted to go dress shopping, and we have to do some food tasting things." My mother said.

"Well, today, I am exhausted and just want to relax."

"I get the feeling you don't want to get married." My mother said.

"No, I just want to chill today. We have a lot of time to get that done." I told her, leaving her in the living room.

I got in our bed and went straight to sleep.

Jade

"Once he touched me, I knew he had won. No one was going to believe me." I said, reading a piece of my book out loud. This treatment center had been therapeutic for me. Last time, I was there for drug treatment, and I didn't realize the root of my problems, but this time, things were different; I was able to get therapy. I bonded with an older woman, named Jane, who was in a similar situation. She killed her ex and her sister because she caught them in bed together. Her family had cut her off, and she had no one. I promised her that, once we both got out of here, she would have a friend in me forever.

My doctor, Dr. Crane, was amazing. He got me to see things a lot clearer. I felt bad that I killed Jared, but I couldn't bring him back, and at that point, I realized that I truly just snapped. He knew that he was gay all that time, and instead of keeping it real with me and being true to himself, he would rather play both sides, and now his ass was dead. Dr. Crane also helped me realize that modeling wasn't that much of a passion and that I just replaced it with another addiction, and he was right. When I modeled I felt like I was on a high, similar to how I felt when I was on drugs. Writing about my life also had been therapeutic. I also asked my family and Briah not to visit me, because I didn't want to get distracted.

Briah

At first, I was mad that Quan and Mel showed up at my house, but when I saw Kay and Mel walking down the stairs, I was happy. She needed to get away from Derrick. I didn't understand why her parents liked him so much. I never really cared for him, and when Melo told me about his suspicions of Derrick abusing her, I believed it. Kayla hadn't been herself since she started messing with him. I felt bad that Kayla had lost her memory, but it felt good to have my friend back.

I was sitting at work, waiting for Angel's call. She had hired a private investigator to watch Jackie, because once I saw the information on the dating site, I passed it along to Angel. The only person I felt bad for was 3, because he was a sweet man, and he, damn sure, didn't deserve the shit Jackie was doing. My phone rang, and I, quickly answered, nervous to hear what Angel had to say.

"Hello." I answered.

"Hey, Briah. I just got off the phone with the PI. This bitch is crazy as hell, if she thinks she is marrying my father. For one, the heffa is still married according to the PI. She's married to a man name Jacob Morgan, who's 75, and currently in a coma. He supposedly slipped and fell. She was under investigation, but they couldn't find anything to tie her to it. Apparently, Mr. Morgan was going broke, so Miss Jackie took out a 20 million dollar life insurance policy on him. My guess is that she wanted him to die, and then, find the next older man to eat off of." Angel explained.

"I can't believe it, I knew something was up. I just hate that I have to break it to him."

"My dad is strong. He'll be fine. Just put it all on me. I am fine with taking the blame. I have to go. Keep me posted." She said, hanging up.

I knew that 3T would be in the office a little later, but time seemed to go slow. I couldn't wait for him to get here, so I could tell him everything that Angel told me. I was happy that Jackie was going to get what she deserved with her stuck up ass and fucked up attitude.

3T walked in a few hours later, with Jackie following right behind him. I rolled my eyes, because I didn't know how I was going tell him the news with this troll following behind him.

"Hey, Briah. Can you order some Chinese food for me and Jackie, and if you want something, get whatever you like." He offered.

"Why can't she just go get it? The food will come faster." Jackie said.

"Why don't you go get the damn food?" I snapped.

"You see how the help talks to me." She said, rolling her eyes.

"I am not the help; I work for 3, and I am his friend." I said.

"All that will end once I become Mrs. Thomas. All of that will change." Jackie bragged.

"Ladies, lets relax." 3T said, coming in between us.

"I was being nice. It's Jackie that always waltzing in here, with an unnecessary attitude."

"Jackie, you was wrong for calling her the help, and Briah, Jackie is going to be my wife, so I need you two to get along."

"Again, why do I need to get along with the help?" Jackie said.

I was done with her. I was going to wait until she left to break the news, but now, I was going to burst her bubble.

"Actually, it's not even a big deal, because I know you guys can't get married." I said, chuckling.

"What are you talking about?" 3T said, looking confused.

"Angel, just called and told me that little missy is married to a man name Jacob Morgan."

"That's crazy." 3T said.

I told him everything that Angel had told me. The look on Jackie's face told it all.

"So, you was using me?" He asked her.

"No, it wasn't even like that. I love you." Jackie said.

"You don't love me; you loved my money!" He spat.

"This is all your fault!" Jackie yelled, charging at me.

Before she had a chance to hit me, I punched her in the face, and she grabbed my hair. 3T grabbed Jackie, as she held on to my hair.

"Get off my hair, bitch!" I spat, as I continued to punch her in the face, until security came upstairs and broke us up.

"Jackie, get the fuck out!" 3T shouted.

"You're going to pay for this shit, bitch!" she said, trying to get at me.

Security escorted her out, and I looked at 3T, and he looked sad. I felt bad for him, because he was really in love with her.

"Are you okay?" I asked, concerned.

"What you think? I can't believe you and Angel was investigating her."

"We just was looking out for you. Something wasn't right."

"I didn't ask for the help."

"Well, you know what, next time, no one will care." I said, rolling my eyes.

He was upset with us when we were the ones looking out for him.

"I am going in my office." He said, walking through and slamming the door.

I understood that he was hurt, but taking out his frustrations on me was wrong, because I was only looking out for him. I went in the bathroom and fixed a few strands of my hair that Jackie pulled. When I went back into the office, 3T was sitting on top of my desk.

"Look, 3, I am really not in the mood to hear any more crap, especially, when I had your back, not to mention, the bitch pulled my hair, which isn't fake!" I snapped.

"I know, and I thought about all that, and I am sorry. I shouldn't have taken my anger out on you, especially, when you were only looking out for me."

"You're right." I said.

"I need a drink, so come with me." He said, inviting me.

"Sure, I need one too. It's been a crazy day." I joked. We went to the bar across from the office; we both needed to release our frustrations. We sat at the bar, and 3 ordered his usual, Jack on the rocks, and I settled for some henny and coke.

"I can't believe that bitch played me. The one time I date my actual race, I get played." 3 joked.

"It happens to the best of us." I said, trying to lighten up the mood.

"I am serious. My mother hated Angel's mother, because she wasn't black, and then, my second wife was always accused of being a gold digger. My mother told me to find a black girl. They don't take your money, but you know what's funny?" He asked.

"What?" I said, curiously.

"Neither one of my wives were after my money." He said, drinking his drink.

3T vented to me, and the whole time, I dreamt of what life would be like with him. After his fifth drink, I knew it was time to go home. He was slurring words and saying off the wall shit.

"3, I think it's time to go home." I said.

"I am trying to go home with you." He said.

"Yeah, okay, let's get you home." I told him.

"I'mma crash at your place. Shit, I brought it." he bragged.

"Whatever, come on." I said.

We walked back to the building the law office was in and got in my car. By the time we pulled up in front of my door, he was snoring. It took me over 30 minutes to get him in the house. Dolores must've heard the commotion, because she came downstairs.

"Briah, what in the hell is going on?" She asked.

"Somebody had a little too much to drink." I told her.

"Sir, you are too grown for this shit." She spat.

"Mind your business." He said, plopping on the couch. "Mind ya' fucking business." He said at her.

I was nervous because Lord knows Dolores could go on for hours.

"I don't know who your black ass talking to, but I'mma go back upstairs, and let you live. I don't feel like beating a nigga ass today." She said, going back up the stairs. I tried to hold in my laughter.

"Who the fuck was that?" He asked.

"Quan's grandmother. Now, sleep it off." I told him, leaving and going upstairs.

The next morning, I woke up to go check on 3T, and he was sitting at the kitchen table, drinking coffee and checking emails, while Dolores made breakfast.

"Good morning." I said, to everyone

"Hey, Briah. Morning." He said.

"I see you two are getting along." I said.

"We're fine, as long as he watches his damn mouth." Dolores said.

"He had a long day." I told her.

"I don't care. Well, I take that back. You know I'm nosey. What happened?" She asked, sitting down.

3T told her the entire rundown with Jackie.

"Well, thank God, you dodged that bullet. She could've killed you next. Shit, you too fine to die." she said, laughing.

"Oh, you think I am fine." He said, smirking.

"Oh, please, negro. You okay." She said.

"No, you said I was fine. You okay, yourself, with that fat ass." He said.

"I know your disrespectful ass ain't talking about my ass. Shit, you wouldn't know what to do with all this ass. I am sure that none of those bitches you messed with could hold a candle to me. Shit, I am pushing 60, and I look damn good." She bragged.

"That you do." He said, licking his lips.

"Mommy?" I heard Chance call out. Thank God I was saved from their flirting session.

I admit, I had a crush on 3T, but he was too old and he treated me like I nothing more than a niece or daughter. At that very moment, I didn't want to cross those boundaries.

Jade

It had been a long road to recovery, but I felt better than ever. I was actually going to get another therapist to see, regularly. It felt good to talk to someone, daily. I was also diagnosed with bipolar 2, a mild case of bipolar, and although it wasn't as strong as having bipolar, I was still going to get the proper treatment for it. Walking out the treatment center, I felt refreshed. When I got outside, I ran straight to Ricky and gave him a big hug.

"Ricky!" I exclaimed.

"Hey, sis, you look so good." He said, smiling.

"Thanks, I feel good, too." I said getting into his car.

"So, sis, what's next?" He asked.

"I've had so much time. You just don't understand, I thought about a lot of shit."

"I hope everything helped you with a clear head." he told me.

"Yes, I am actually going to quit modeling. I have to call Scott."

"Oh, boy is in love with you." Ricky said.

"Yeah, right."

"Trust me. He called me so much and every time I told him the same thing." Ricky said, laughing.

"He probably just wanted to see how I was doing. Give me your phone." I said.

Ricky gave me his phone, and I dialed Scott; he answered on the first ring.

"Jade, I hope this is you." He said.

"It is." I said, smiling through the phone.

"I am so happy to hear from you. I am catching the next flight there." He said.

"Slow down, Mister." I said, laughing.

"Look, Jade. I missed you; I want to be there for you."

"And, you will, because I'll be in Cali in two days." I told him.

Ricky looked at me. I hadn't told anyone, but I was moving back to California; Atlanta just had too much drama for me.

"Okay, I'll pick you up from the airport then."

"Okay." I said, hanging up.

"Since, you just got home." Ricky said.

"What is home?" I asked.

"Where ever you feel at peace." he replied.

"Well, we both know how much peace I feel here." I said, sarcastically.

"True, so what you going do out there?" He asked.

"I still have my condo. I just finished my book, and I have a meeting with a network." I told him.

"Reality TV, sis?" he asked.

"Not like that." I said, laughing.

"Well, good, I need somewhere sunny to visit".

We laughed and joked, until we pulled up to Ricky's house.

"Savannah made you a huge feast."

"Good, cause that treatment center food taste like shit." I said, laughing, getting out the car.

Ricky opened the door and there were balloons everywhere, and a welcome home banner; tears slowly fell down, as I realized how loved I truly was.

"Bitchhhhh." Briah said, running up to me.

"What are you doing here?" I asked.

"I couldn't miss my friend's welcome home dinner, and look who I brought." She said, turning around, and Kayla turned the corner.

"Hi, Jade." She said, smiling.

"Come here, Kay. You know I like hugs, with your stuck up ass." I said, grabbing her in an embrace.

"Come in the dining room." Briah said.

I walked in the dining room and Savanah, Ricky, my grandparents, and parents were sitting at the table.

"Mommy." I said, not caring about the tears that were falling.

"Come here, baby." She said, crying too.

We hugged for a long time and just cried. I didn't care about the past; I just wanted my mother back. After our emotional reunion, I sat down, and we all ate and talked. This was the first time, in years, that I actually felt good about life.

After dinner, Kayla and Briah grabbed me, and we went and sat on Ricky's back porch.

"I got a case of the thotritas." Briah, said laughing.

"That used to be our shit." I said.

"Nah, it used to be y'all shit." Kayla said.

"Whatever, heffa." I said, mushing her.

Briah and I opened ours, and Kayla looked at us.

"Umm, missy, you better drink this. I ain't bring any Pinot." Briah said, laughing.

"I drink Patron." she said, rolling her eyes.

"Yeah, that's how Melo got in those draws." Briah said, causing me to spit my drink out.

"Thanks, Briah, just put my business out there." She said, rolling her eyes.

"It's cool. Melo is fine, as hell. I don't blame you, but what's up with this wedding?" I asked.

"It's still going on; I am just conflicted." Kayla admitted.

"Why?" I asked.

"Because, I still don't have my memory, and I don't love Derrick. I am in love with Melo." Kayla admitted.

"Well, you're still young. Go for what you want. Shit, look how long it took me to live for me." I told her, giving her advice.

"You right. I just don't know what to do."

"Kayla, do what's best for Kayla and Kayla only." Jade told her.

The rest of the night, we sat back and reminisced about the good old days and promised that we would never allow anything to cause us to stop speaking. It felt good to have my college friends back.

A few days later, I was leaving Atlanta for good. I would probably visit my brother and the girls, but I was never making it my address again. Before my parents left, I reconnected with my mother, and she promised to make a trip to Cali soon. It felt good to rebuild my relationship with my mother, because at the end of the day, every girl needed their mother. Just as promised, Scott was waiting for me at the airport when our eyes locked. We both started smiling.

"Damn, girl. You look good." He said, hugging me.

"Thanks. You're not looking so bad yourself." I told him.

"I know you like what you see." He said, opening the door for me.

During the car ride home, I briefed him on my plans, and I was happy that he understood that modeling wasn't for me. I needed to do things that was beneficial to my health.

Six months later ...

Kayla

"A week away, can you believe it?" Briah said, laying on her couch. We were at her house, chilling before I became a married woman.

"I know, I am so nervous." I admitted.

"Don't be. You're making the right decision, remember?" She said, taunting me, because just three weeks ago, she asked was I making a smart decision, and I told her not to worry about me, because I was making the right decision.

"I didn't forget. Anyway, have you spoken to Jade? I really need to see how she looks in her dress." I said, changing the subject.

"Yes. Jade said she would be here by tomorrow, so don't worry." Briah assured me.

"Okay, good."

"Don't worry. We'll have some strippers the night before."

"No we won't. My mother said, a southern woman takes a nice hot bath with a glass of wine and relax before her big day." I said.

"Kayla, grow the fuck up. Damn!" Briah snapped, getting off the couch and answering the doorbell.

She opened it and Quan, Chance, and Melo walked in. I had been avoiding Melo since our slip-up and was doing a good job, until now.

"Hey boogie girl." Quan said. I stuck my middle finger up at him, because he loved to fuck with me.

"Auntie Kay." Chance squealed, running over and hugging me.

"Hey, baby." I said, smiling. Chance brought me so much joy.

"I would have loved an invite to the wedding." Quan said, plopping on the couch.

"Briah had a plus one."

"And, I chose, Dolores. Nobody wants Quan's ghetto ass there. I needed to bring someone classy." She said.

"Now, I love D, but ain't shit classy about her." I said, joking.

"Don't be talking about my grandmother. Matter of fact, Briah let me holla at you in the kitchen. Mel, after I am done, we can be out." Quan said, walking to the kitchen.

"So, you can fuck me, but can't speak." Melo spat.

"Really, Melo? It's been six months. You know I'm getting married." I told him.

"Yeah, that's what your mind tells you, but not your heart." He said.

"Whatever. It's what my parents want." I told him.

"Unbelievable! I sure hope you grow the fuck up one day. How you going to marry someone, and you still didn't get your memory back. Man, you're the dumbest broad I ever met in my fucking life. That nigga was beating your ass so bad that you tried to kill yourself. That's why you don't have a fucking memory, but Kayla on some real shit, I am done with your stupid ass. First, it was that nigga, Jason. Now, it's this whack nigga. I am a real man and deserve a real woman who don't do shit for their parents, but instead she do for herself. Good luck on the wedding. I hope he doesn't beat your ass, again." He snapped, walking out and slamming the door.

His words really hurt me. I had tears rolling down my eyes. I wanted to believe that Derrick was this great guy, but I, definitely, couldn't deny the fact that I did get creeped out in his presence. Briah and Quan came out laughing and joking, until they saw me crying.

"Kay, what happened?" Briah asked

"Melo probably got tired of chasing her." Quan joked.

"Leave me alone, Quan!" I yelled.

"Man, go yell at that nigga you marrying. I'm out." He said, leaving.

"Briah, tell the truth. Was Derrick abusing me?" I asked.

"I am not sure; you never told me, but there were signs. He was very possessive, and we didn't hang out like we used to." She admitted.

"I don't know what to do." I cried.

"Put on your big girl panties, and get what you deserve." Briah told me.

What Briah and Melo said weighed heavy on me; I didn't know what to believe. I left Briah's house and drove straight home. When I got there, Derrick was there, and I wanted to pick his brain a little bit to see what his side was.

"Hey, babe." He said, smiling and kissing me on the cheek.

I, immediately, got creeped out. "Derrick, I was wondering how we were before my accident?" I asked.

"We were good; I mean we argued and shit, but we was good." He said.

"Why didn't Melo allow you in the room until I woke up?" I asked.

"I don't know. To be honest, I thought you was cheating on me with him." He told me.

"Well, I can't remember anything, and this shit is driving me crazy." I confessed.

"Don't worry. Once we're married, and you hear my vows, all those beautiful memories will come right back." He said, kissing me on my forehead. I was happy that he had confidence, because I didn't.

It was the day of my wedding, and I had this uneasy feeling. I was in the hotel, sitting at the vanity, admiring my makeup, when there was a knock at the door.

"Come in." I said.

"Hey boo. We're going to drive to the church in about twenty minutes." She said.

"Okay." I told her.

"Kayla, I love you to death, but you damn sure aren't acting like someone who's getting married in an hour."

"I know. I just wish I could get my damn memory back." I said, frustrated.

"Boo, it will come back. Don't worry." She assured me.

I slipped on a Maxi dress and grabbed my wedding dress. We got into our car service and drove to the church. Briah was talking to me, but I wasn't paying attention to anything she was saying; I was in my own world. Briah was talking when we heard a loud boom, and I hit my head on the car seat.

"Ouch." I cried.

"Kayla, are you okay?" Briah asked.

"Give me a second." I said, laying back.

"Sorry, ladies, my breaks stop working on me." The driver said.

"Okay, how long do we have? She's getting married." Briah told him.

"Don't worry. I already spoke with my boss, and he's sending someone to pick you ladies up."

"God is trying to stop this wedding." Briah joked.

"I think he is, too." I said, as I began getting bits and pieces of my life back.

My mind flashed back to Melo and his son walking into my class on the first day, as well as, countless times Derrick raped and abused me.

"Kayla, are you okay? You're over there, staring into space." Briah said.

"I am not marrying Derrick. I remember everything." I said in tears.

"Stop fucking crying. Fuck him."

"You're right; it's time to do me." I said, just as the car serviceman told us his coworker was out there. We got out the car, and I gave the car service guy Melo's address.

"Bri, he's going to drop me off where I belong. I want you to go to the church and tell Derrick's punk ass that I remember everything, and this bullshit wedding is off. And, tell my parents, if they can't accept my decision, to enjoy Texas." I told her.

I had found the confidence I needed and prayed Melo gave me another chance, because this was the last time I would ever in life make him feel like he was coming second to another person. If my parents couldn't accept him, then, it was time for me to love them from a distance. The car service guy dropped me off, and instead of ringing Melo's bell, I banged on it like the police and prayed that he was home. I banged on his door for the next five minutes, until it flew open.

Melo was standing in front of me, shirtless, and looking good.

"What the hell you want, Kayla?" He said.

"I want you, Mel. No games. I want all of you. I remember everything." I told him.

"Well, I told you I was done with that back and forth shit." He spat.

"Please, Mel, we're bigger than this." I pleaded.

"Nah, you good." He said.

"Mel, who's that?" I heard a woman say, as she came to the door, wrapping her arms around his waist.

"It's like that, Mel." I said, trying to fight tears.

"Yup." He said, slamming the door in my face.

I was crushed; I had definitely messed up for good.

Epilogue

Jade

It felt good to get my story out there; I had just finished filming an episode of Iyanla Vanzant, "Fix My Life", and not only did she help me, but she help me put missing pieces together with my family. My book had become a best seller, and I was beyond proud of myself.

"Babe, take my hand." Scott said, grabbing my hand, as we walked on the beach.

Scott and I had been together since I moved back to Cali. We had been working together more, and he helped me rebuild. I rubbed my stomach and smiled, because Scott and I were expanding our family. I was seven months pregnant, with a little boy, and we were engaged to get married. I wasn't focused on anything but my family. I wasn't addicted to anything. Just high off life.

Briah

"Chance, slow down!" I yelled, as he ran off to Quan while we were in the park.

"Chill out. My little nigga going be a football star." Quan said, laughing.

"Well, I'd rather not call him a nigga." I said, rolling my eyes.

Quan and I were doing great, co-parenting. He left the drug game alone and was doing real estate. He spent a lot of time with Chance, which I loved, because I wanted my son to have his father in his life. Quan refused to talk to Black, and I didn't press the issue. Quan's grandmother moved down here, for good, especially, when her and 3T became serious. I still work for him, and the feelings I thought I had for him went away. I was just living my life and taking care of my son.

Kayla

"This is definitely the house I want." I told the real estate agent.

"Great choice. Come in the kitchen, so you guys can sign the papers." She said, looking at Melo and me and smiling.

"This is, definitely, the fresh start that we deserve." I told him.

"You're right about that." He said, kissing my forehead and rubbing my stomach. I was five months pregnant and having a baby girl. The day I went to Melo's house, I wouldn't leave until he admitted his true feelings for me. Once he did that, the girl who was there left with an attitude, and Carmelo and I begin rebuilding. We, definitely, agreed that we needed a new house to start fresh. We didn't waste any time when we got back together. A month after that, we went to City Hall and got married. My parents refused to speak to me, and unlike in the past, I was, perfectly, fine with that. Briah told me that she told everyone why the wedding was off, but they still insisted that I should have married Derrick. After that, I knew it was time to just cut my losses. Now, I was happier than I had ever been. Some say Love don't last anyway, but in my case, it did.

Coming Soon

Untitled

Waking up with a headache wasn't in my plans. I wasn't ready for my reality once my eyes were exposed to sunlight. I pulled the covers off of my body and saw an extra set of legs. I took a deep breath and turned to my side, coming face-to-face with Chris, the fine ass construction worker from last night. I closed my eyes, instead of screaming and kicking him out. My luck with men was horrible; I felt that I had everything going for me. I was beautiful, smart, had a career, was funny, and no kids. Everyone thought I was lucky, but I was missing something... a companion. Here I was, 28, and I hadn't even begun to think about marriage. My friends either had children or were getting married, and I envied them, mostly, because I was going be that old ass lady with thirty cats.

I had always craved for a relationship, but maybe that was my problem. To me, a man would complete me. I also had way too many rules, according to my friends, but to me, you know what you want when you want it. You had to be over 30, I didn't want a teeny bopper, a coming to age 20 something, or a baby; I wanted mature man. You must have a car, live alone, no kids, big penis, perfect body, great lover, a job, and handsome. I was slightly praying for Idris Elba to come swoop me off my feet. First, there was Eric, he was cute, had a decent job, but no car, and he wanted me to play taxi. I just couldn't respect a grown ass man who expected me to be driving Mr. Daisy. Let's not forget about Dane; the smooth talker, with hazel eyes. Every time you asked him where he worked, he always was "waiting for his papers". Papers for what Negro. You were born here. Immigration was not looking for you.

I am sorry, but I am not here for a thirty year old bum. Of course, there was Dominic, the fine ass businessman, wealthy, great job, owned his own car, and house. I was in love during the dating, until he dropped the 'I have a kid' speech, which killed my mood. I refused to deal with baby mama drama. I had dealt with that in the past, and I was way passed that. Let's not forget Jessie, he had a decent job, charm, and good looks. His head game was amazing, but his penis didn't even tickle me. I couldn't deal with lackluster sex partners. My luck sucked. I think God wanted me to wait for him. Hell, I wish he would come down here and marry me. I could never find a guy who was down for a relationship. If I did, the sex sucked, or he had character flaws, that I just couldn't deal with. And, if the sex was good, he didn't want a relationship. I told myself maybe it's me... It had to be me.

Chapter 1

After kicking Chris out, I began detoxing my house. Now, Chris was cool and all, but unfortunately, I slept with him on the first night, so I knew we wouldn't be speaking again. That was my rule, one night stands was just that? I turned the radio on and began deep cleaning. I was interrupted by a phone call from one of my best friends, Janae.

"Hello."

"Hey, Nat." She said, sounding chipper.

"Was up?"

"What are you doing?"

"Getting my Saturday cleaning done."

"Good, but don't forget about tonight. It's game night." She said, sounding cheerful.

"Listen, Nae, I have to go, but I'll be there." I said, rushing her off the phone.

I loved my friends, but to me, they had the perfect life with their men, whereas, I would, probably, be the fifth wheel at game night. Now, don't get me wrong, my friends and their men never made me feel like that; I made myself feel like that.

Later that night...

After my day of cleaning and self-pity, it was time to get dressed. I choose a simple, low-cut biker, Levis, a black tee, sneaker wedges, and a MK watch. My hair was in a sexy shoulder length bob; I adorned my face, with no makeup, instead opting for Revlon pink lip gloss. I sprayed Rihanna's newest fragrance and was out the door. It took me about twenty minutes to reach Janae's house. I lived in a condo, and Janae and her husband had just purchased a beautiful house. I pulled in their driveway and walked up the stairs. Before I could ring the bell, I was greeted by my beautiful god daughter, Chloe.

Chloe was everyone's baby, but I had a special bond with her. She was the cutest five year old I had ever met.

"Auntie Nat." She screeched, almost knocking my bottle of wine out my hand.

"Hey, baby, look at you, all cute and stuff." I said, closing the door behind me.

"Where's you mom and dad?"

"There in the game room, with Aunt Jas and Uncle Mike." She said, skipping to the game room. I could hear Nae yelling at her.

"Chloe, what the hell I tell you about opening the door for people?" She said, walking right into me.

"Hey Nat. Let me take this." Nae said, grabbing my wine to put in the fridge.

I walked into the room to find the men engrossed in a game of chess. I waved to them; I didn't want to interrupt the game, and Jas was behind the bar making drinks.

"I hope you can make a drink girl." I said, scaring her in my All State guy voice."

"Girl, you are crazy. What you want to drink."

"Something good." I said, sitting on the bar stool.

"It's damn near ten, and Santana didn't bring his rotten ass here at" Janae said bitching. Although, Janae was the shortest of the crew, she was the feistiest one. We all liked to call her mama bear.

"Nae, relax. You know Santana never on time." Jas said.

"I don't." Before Janae could get her word out the doorbell ring.

"Looks like we're saved by the bell."

Mike said, ending his game and going to get the door. We all began laughing, because Janae stood their quiet. Janae, Jas, Victor, Santana, Mike, and I were all best friends. Janae, Jas, and I grew up in the same neighborhood, and our parents were all best friends. We met the boys in high school. Janae started dated Mike, Jas started dating Victor, and Santana and I were just friends. I was sipping my drink in my own thoughts, when Santana walked in. He was the playboy out the group and craved attention. Now, don't get me wrong. Santana was fine, but I could never get with his antics. Santana stood at six one, he was very slender, light skin, with nice wavy hair. His smile could get a woman's panties at any point, and that was his problem. He was also very flashy and an up and coming singer who got everything he wanted, or so he thought.

"Well, hello, ladies." Santana said, winking at me.

He walked to the bar, hugged Jas, gave me a hug, and tried to grab my ass. Before I stopped him, he walked right pass Jas, dabbing the fellas.

"I just know this nigga didn't walk in my fucking house and not speak."

"Babe, chill." Mike said.

Santana and Janae hadn't got along since the day he picked up Chloe with his crazy ex, whom then tried to kill both of them. Once the tension was gone, everyone began having fun, drinking reminiscing. Mike, Santana, Jas, and I began playing spades. While Nae and Vic looked on. After our game, Vic stood up. He was the quiet one out of the group. Victor was also my brother; not real brother, but he was as close as it came. There were things my girls didn't know about me that he knew. Vic was a professional football player who played for the New Jersey Acers. He was a big deal to his fans, but to us, he was family.

"Listen, y'all. We have known each other for damn near thirteen years. Y'all are my family, and now I want to share with you all how I been feeling." He began speaking, walking towards Jas getting on one knee.

"Jasmine Alexa Harris, you have been there with me through it all. I love you to death. Will you marry me?" He said, proposing to Jas.

I was happy for them, but I know an eye rolled popped out. Why couldn't I be getting married? Jas said yes, as she began crying, and everyone was truly happy for them. I was happy, but unfortunately, my own issues wouldn't allow me to be a real friend to them.

"Look, guys. I enjoyed myself, but I gotta go home and give my fiancé some good love." Jas said, winking her eye, hugging us all.

Once they left, Santana grabbed the Hennessey and had us taking shot after shot.

"Ayo, Santana. We are not in college anymore." Mike said, slurring his words.

"Nigga, in college, you couldn't handle shots. Remember those twins in college." Santana said, laughing.

"No, what twins?" Janae said, becoming angry.

"Baby, it was nothing. You know I didn't mess with anyone." Mike said, trying to kiss her.

"Mess with the couch. Goodnight, Natalia." She said, leaving the room.

"Why must you have a big ass mouth?" Mike said, playfully hitting his shoulder, walking out.

"And, then there were two." Santana said, smiling.

"Why the hell you do that?"

"Because, Nae always in my shit, so I figured I would fuck with her." He said, taking a swig from the bottle. "Let's finish playing the question game."

For the rest of the night, I was actually enjoying Santana's Company.

"Whoa." I said, standing up, feeling my head spin.

I knew I was drunk, because the room began spinning. Luckily for me, Janae and Mike had a guest room within the game room, because there was no way I was driving. As I began undressing, I could feel someone undressing me with their eyes, so I turned around and there was Santana, smiling licking his lips.

"Oh, no, Santana." I said, covering my breast.

"Damn, Nattie, your body is banging." He said, admiring my body.

"Don't be shy." Santana said, walking towards me, kissing my neck, getting me all hot and bothered. No one knew, but Santana and I were each other's first sexual experience. It was prom night, and we both wanted to do it and get it over with.

"Auntie, wake up." I heard, as Chloe was rocking my arm back in forth.

Opening my eyes, I was met with Chloe's adorable self. She had two long pigtails, and Doc Mcstuffin pajamas.

"Give me a second." I said, moving my legs.

I felt another set of legs and figured that this had to be a dream or déjà vu. I had this same dream, yesterday, but it wasn't a dream, and Chloe was in it. I realized it wasn't a dream when Janae walked in.

"Natalia Bridgeport. What the hell is wrong with you? Why is Santana lying next to you?" She shouted, angrily.

"Mama, you said a bad word." Chloe said, laughing.

"Chloe, go to your room."

Before I could get out of bed, I realized I didn't have any clothes on, so I took the sheet to cover myself.

"Don't cover yourself, now, sleeping with the devil in my house." I guess, Santana, either woke up, or he was tired of hearing her talking shit.

"Man, Janae, all you do is bitch. Shut the fuck up." he said, getting out of bed, showing his naked behind.

"Cover that shit up. You know what, I don't want you in my house!" She yelled.

"Good, that's why I am getting dress. I am surprised Mike married you. All you do is nag.

Mike walked in, hearing all the commotion, and when he realized what was going on, he started laughing.

"I knew one day this was going happen." He said, as he clapped his hands.

"Mike, you find this shit funny. I want more for my friend." She said, looking at me in disgust.

I had been quiet, but quite frankly, I was tired of her mouth.

"Look, Nae. I am grown, and I am sorry for sleeping with him in your house, but I am not sorry for what I did. Can you guys give me some privacy? I want to get home." I said, closing my eyes.

Before Nae could finish, Mike grabbed her and walked out the room. Santana looked at me and smiled.

"Sheesh, Nattie, that shit was amazing."

"Well, thank you. Wasn't so bad, yourself." I said, smiling back, slipping my jeans on.

"Listen, I am out, but I will be calling you." He said, kissing my forehead and leaving.

I felt butterflies and laid back on the bed, so I could gather my thoughts, wondering if I really have feelings for Santana.

Text Shan to 22828 to stay up to date with new releases, sneak peeks, contest, and more...

Check your spam if you don't receive an email thanking you for signing up.